AT CROSS PURPOSES

P.F. FORD

Copyright © 2022 P.F. Ford

All rights reserved.

This is a work of fiction. All characters, places and events in this book are either a product of the author's imagination or are used fictitiously. Any resemblance to real life counterparts is purely coincidental.

No part of this book may be reproduced in any form or by any electronic or mechanical means, including information storage and retrieval systems, without written permission from the author, except for the use of brief quotations in a book review.

Cover design by Bespoke Book Covers

For Suzanne

CHAPTER 1

Monday

It was 08:00 as Flutter put a lead on Winston, his rather odd looking dog, and prepared to leave the small house they now called home.

'Are you ready?' he asked the dog.

The dog looked up with his big, sad eyes.

'Oh, no. Not the sad eyes again,' said Flutter. 'I understand you're missing the big house, but there are benefits to this place. It's cosier for a start and, whilst I understand you're missing the enormous garden, the park's only two minutes away. I think you'll find a leisurely stroll around there every morning before we go to the office will be far more enjoyable than walking along all those streets into town. You'll even have time to stop and sniff stuff without me hurrying you along.'

The dog managed a solitary wag of his tail.

'That's more like it,' said Flutter. 'Trust me, you're going to love it here. In a couple of weeks, you'll have forgotten the other place.'

He led the dog out to the street, pulled the door closed and together they took the short walk to the park gates.

'Here we go,' said Flutter. 'Didn't I tell you it wasn't far?'

The old dog's tail wagged furiously as he strained forward, eager to explore the park, and Flutter bent down to unclip the lead from the dog's collar.

'Now remember, I'm trusting you to behave yourself and not run off.'

Winston gave him a look that suggested such an idea was preposterous and shambled off to sniff at the base of the nearest tree.

Flutter had never had a dog before, and had never even considered owning one, but Winston was inherited and, in just a few short weeks, the dog had captured his heart. Now he couldn't imagine life without a dog, and he watched with pride as Winston headed away.

Short, stocky legs and a long body caused Winston to roll from side to side as he moved, turning his walk into something more akin to a waddle, and making the word "graceful" redundant to anyone wishing to describe his movement. In addition to his body shape, Winston's huge, dangly ears hinted at the possibility of Basset Hound ancestry, but if this was indeed the case, those pedigree genes had been well-diluted by the time of his birth.

As Winston sniffed around the tree, Flutter ambled ahead along the path towards the narrow river that wound its way through the park. This early, it was quiet in the park and he soon became lost in his thoughts. He had come back to Waterbury seeking a new start and a quiet life, but so much had happened in the first few weeks after he had been released from prison there had been a point where he was wondering if he'd done the right thing.

At least things had calmed down after that, but now they were too quiet. He and local journalist Katie Donald were hoping to work together as private investigators, but there's a big difference between hoping to do something and actually doing it, and now, two weeks into the venture, they were still waiting for their first job!

As Flutter led Winston towards the front door of his tiny, terraced house an hour later, he reflected on his decision to forgo the spacious luxury of the house he had been left by his father. The more times he did this, the more he came to believe he had done the right thing.

In the short time he'd been at the big house, there had been nothing but trouble, whereas life had been trouble free since he had moved into the terraced house. Yes, it had been in a state when he moved in, but now, after a lot of hard work, it was almost finished. Clean, warm and cosy, as far as Flutter was concerned, it was the perfect home.

As he opened the front door, he saw a letter on his doormat. This was a surprise because the postman rarely came before mid-morning, so that meant it had been hand-delivered. He knew it couldn't be personal correspondence as no-one he knew was aware of his address, so he assumed it was junk mail.

As he carried it through to his kitchen, he turned the envelope over and experienced a moment of panic that stopped him in his tracks. There was something about the typeface, layout, and logo that reminded him of the official prison service letters he knew only too well. He took a couple of deep breaths to calm himself.

'Come on, Flutter,' he said out loud. 'You can't go through this every time a letter arrives. You've done your time, you've got a release letter, and you've kept your nose clean. If you were in trouble, they wouldn't write and tell you, would they? Of course not. They'd send half a dozen big, hairy-arsed coppers to drag you away. Now, pull yourself together and let's see what this is about.'

Impressed by the positivity behind his personal pep talk, Flutter made his way through to the kitchen and placed the letter to one side as he attended to the more pressing matter of feeding Winston. Only when the old dog had buried his face in his bowl did Flutter slit the envelope open.

As he unfolded the letter, he could see it was from the Probation Service. This was both concerning, and puzzling, as he wasn't on probation. He sat down and read through the letter in growing disbelief. When he got to the end, he cursed in vividly colourful tones.

'Bloody 'ell, Winston,' he said. 'I've been stitched up. They say there's been an administrative error and I should have been fixed up with a local probation supervisor when I came out.'

The dog looked up at Flutter and wagged his tail.

'Don't wag your tail, mate. It's not good news. It appears I'm now officially on probation, although I'm not exactly sure what that means. I've got to call this Mrs Rodgers and arrange a meeting so she can get me started.'

Winston's tail had stopped wagging and now he looked uncertainly at Flutter, who immediately felt guilty and bent down to him.

'Hey, it's okay,' he said, stroking Winston's head. 'It's not your fault. I'm the idiot who mixed with the wrong people, and I'm going to have to toe the line for a bit longer, that's all. Let's just hope they don't make life too difficult. Anyway, it could be worse; at least I haven't been sent back inside.'

Winston acknowledged this positive thought with more enthusiastic tail wagging.

Flutter grabbed his mobile phone, keyed in the number he'd been given in the letter, then changed his mind and put the phone back down. He looked at Winston, who seemed to offer a reproachful look in return.

Flutter sighed.

'Yeah, I suppose you're right, Winston. It won't go away, will it? I might as well bite the bullet and get it over with.'

Reluctantly, he prodded the numbers on his phone, then raised it to his ear as it rang.

'Hello? Is that Mrs Rodgers? My name's Harvey Gamble. You sent me a letter.'

'Ah, Mr Gamble. Thank you for calling. It's very good of you to get back to me so soon.'

'I didn't know how long you'd wait until you called the police and had me dragged in.'

'This isn't the dark ages, Harvey. We only get the police involved as a last resort. I'd like to think we're a bit more enlightened nowadays.'

He couldn't quite put his finger on it, but there was something about the sound of her voice. Slightly seductive, and vaguely familiar, it immediately made him comfortable speaking with her.

'So they won't be knocking my door down anytime soon?'

'Not on our account. We're the ones at fault, which is why I asked you to call me, rather than demanding you come here. I hope you feel that's reasonable?'

Flutter was impressed. He couldn't remember the last time anyone in a position of authority had apologised to him.

'I've got to admit it makes a change from the usual heavy-handed approach.'

'I'm glad you think so. I always try to make the probation experience as pleasant as I can.'

'So, what happens now, then?'

'I appreciate this has probably come as something of a shock as you were released several weeks ago, so I'd like to make our first meeting an informal one.'

'Informal?'

'Our offices are being refurbished right now, and it's all a bit of mess. So, I thought we could meet for a coffee. This way we can ease you in gently, as it were. Do you think that would be okay?'

Flutter had to admit, the more he listened to her voice, the more he liked the idea of Mrs Rodgers easing him in gently.

'Yeah, that sounds fair enough. Have you got somewhere in mind?'

'There's a coffee shop in town called Leslie's.'

'Oh, yeah. I know the one.'

'I suggest we have our first meeting there. We can get to know each other as I explain the rules to you over a coffee. Does that sound okay?'

Flutter thought this definitely sounded like a more enlightened approach than anything he'd ever heard of.

'Yeah. I mean, I'd rather not be doing it at all, but if I've got to do it, your way sounds all right. When do you want to start?'

'Could you make it today?'

'Today? Blimey, that's a bit sudden.'

'I know it's not your fault but, as you can imagine, we're already weeks behind schedule. That's why I'd like to get started sooner rather than later.'

'I had plans,' said Flutter, evasively. 'What time do you have in mind?'

'I should be able to get there at around three, so what if we say three-thirty?'

'What if I'm late?'

'Then I'll have another coffee and wait a little longer.'

'The thing is, I can't guarantee exactly what time I'll be there.'

'I understand this is being arranged at short notice, so it would be unreasonable of me to expect you to be there on the dot, wouldn't it?'

'Yeah, I suppose so. But how will I know it's you?'

'How many women are you expecting to be working on a laptop in Leslie's at that time of the afternoon?'

Flutter couldn't recall seeing anyone using a laptop in Leslie's at any time.

'Right. Fair enough. I'll be there around three-thirty.'

'This is an excellent start,' she said. 'If we can maintain this level of co-operation, we're going to get on very well.'

'The way I see it, I've got no choice, so there's no point fighting you, is there?'

'Try to look at me as your friend, and you'll find the entire process much easier.'

'My friend? Well, I suppose I can try,' said Flutter, doubtfully.

'Good. I'll see you this afternoon.'

'Righto,' he said, but she had already ended the call.

'Right, Winston,' said Flutter, as he put the phone down. 'I'm going to ask Katie to look after you for an hour this afternoon, so you're going to have to promise to behave. That means no sneaky farts from under her desk. Understand?'

Winston yawned expansively, as if bored with the conversation, then turned his back on Flutter and curled into a ball in his bed.

'But what exactly am I going to tell Katie?' muttered Flutter to himself, as he tidied the kitchen. 'Do I tell her the truth? Or should I wait and see how it's going to work before I tell her?'

After a few minutes deliberation, he elected to err on the side of caution. He would go to the meeting and find out how being on probation would affect him before he broke the news to her. Hopefully, it wouldn't affect their plans and she would be okay about it. In the meantime, he would tell her he had an appointment booked with the dentist this afternoon, but he had forgotten to tell her before.

At roughly the time Flutter was discovering the letter on his doormat, Katie Donald was just settling at her desk. She slipped a small mirror from her handbag and gazed at her reflection. She frowned and uttered a sigh at the sight of her pale-face and the growing bags under her eyes. What she wouldn't give for a worry-free week in the sun. But holidays cost money, and that was in short supply which was the cause of the sleepless nights.

There was a solution to the money problem in the form of a large cheque sitting in the top drawer of her desk, but it came with its own set of problems. She had recently been sent the cheque by gangster Jimmy Jewle after finding out what had happened to his nephew.

The cheque was in the top drawer of her desk, but she steadfastly refused to cash it on the grounds it was dirty money. She also had the suspicion if she accepted his money, he would assume she was in his pocket and she had promised herself that would never happen!

The strident sound of her mobile phone rudely interrupted her thoughts. Making a mental note to find a new ringtone, she reached for the phone and smiled as she saw the caller's name on the screen.

'Morning, Flutter,' she said.

'Hi, Katie. How are you?'

'I'm fine. If you're hoping to hear we've got a case to investigate, I'm afraid you're going to be disappointed.'

'Actually, I'm calling to ask a favour.'

'What sort of favour?' she asked suspiciously.

'I've got an appointment at the dentist this afternoon and I'd completely forgotten about it. I couldn't leave Winston with you for an hour, could I?'

'Has he eaten anything I'm going to regret?'

'I've told him sneaky farts are off the menu, if that's what you mean.'

'Yes, but did he take any notice?'

'We won't know that until this afternoon, will we?' said Flutter. 'Come on, you know you love him, really.'

'Oh, all right then.'

'Katie, you're an angel. I'll see you just after three.'

CHAPTER 2

FLUTTER WAS FEELING NERVOUS AND, as he reached Leslie's, he peered through the window, eager to identify the mysterious Mrs Rodgers before he entered the shop. There were only half a dozen customers in the shop, so he couldn't fail to spot the only woman with a laptop open on the table before her.

She was facing him, with a mobile phone pressed to her ear, but was bent over the table, making notes on a pad. Her long, dark hair had tumbled forward, making it impossible for him to see her face, but somehow he felt a little more at ease just knowing where she was sitting.

He took a deep breath, pushed the door open, walked into the shop, and headed for the counter to order his coffee. He kept his eye on Mrs Rodgers, but her head was still bowed down, and as he took his coffee and headed for her table, she still seemed unaware he had arrived.

As he reached her, she barely glanced up, but pointed to the chair opposite her with her pen, then covered the phone for a second.

'Take a seat,' she said. 'I won't be a minute.'

Flutter sat down and watched the woman. He had yet to get a clear view of her face, but there was something about her that seemed vaguely familiar, although he couldn't put his finger on exactly what it was.

At last, she finished her call, placed the phone on the table, made one last note, and placed her pen down next to the phone. Then she used her two forefingers to push her long hair back behind her ears, and as she sat back and smiled, it all came rushing back to him.

He stared at her face, his mouth open, lost for words.

'Hallo, Harvey,' she said with a smile. 'You look surprised to see me.'

Flutter's brain had suddenly turned to mush, and his mouth flapped wordlessly. Jenny Blake had been Flutter's first and only serious girlfriend.

'Surprised?' he said, finally. 'Blimey, Jenny, I didn't think I'd ever see you again.'

'You mean after you ran off and left me without saying a word?'

Flutter squirmed uncomfortably.

'It was a spur-of-the-moment thing. I had to leave. I just couldn't take it anymore.'

'You didn't even say goodbye!'

'I seem to recall you dumped me. You told me we were finished.'

'You dumped me first,' she said. 'You ditched me for a girl with big boobs. Or have you forgotten?'

Flutter didn't need reminding. Even now, fifteen years later, he could vividly recall how he had given in to temptation, then been tossed aside once the other girl got what she wanted. He had dumped Jenny after going steady with her for 18 months, just to become a notch on a bedpost. How stupid was that?

'No, I haven't forgotten. It was the worst decision of my life. I must have told you that a thousand times after we got back together.'

'Probably two thousand,' she said. 'It got boring in the end.'

'You got your own back, though, didn't you?'

'I certainly did. You thought I'd taken you back because I had forgiven you. You should have known—'

'Yeah, hell hath no fury, right?' finished Flutter. 'So, why would I say goodbye after that?'

'But we were even after that,' she said. 'The slate was clean, level playing field, and all that.'

'You really think it would have worked like that?' he asked. 'Two wrongs would have made a right?'

'I don't know, but I was willing to try.'

'How was I supposed to know that if you didn't say?'

'My plan was to let you stew for a few weeks and suffer like I did, then I would tell you. But you cleared off before I got the chance.'

'Yeah, well, I was young and lonely, and brokenhearted. How could I possibly have known you planned to do that?'

There was an awkward silence as she pulled a file from a briefcase on the seat next to her, set it down carefully on the table and flipped it open. As she looked at what Flutter assumed were his case notes, he sipped at his coffee. Having got over his initial surprise, he was now feeling a lot more confident about the situation and he looked up at her with a cheeky grin.

'Even though your, er, you know,' he used his hands to indicate his chest, 'weren't as big, you had much nicer legs,' he said. 'Beautiful, they were. Long, and slender...'

She looked questioningly, but Flutter misunderstood her meaning.

'I'm sure they still are,' he said, keen not to offend. 'I didn't mean to suggest—'

'Yes, thank you, that's enough of that.'

'I'm just saying. Unfortunately, I was too young to realise it back then, but I'm older now and I appreciate that sometimes less is more, you kn—'

'Let's just remember why we're here, shall we?' she said sternly. 'Our relationship, such as it is, will be strictly professional, nothing more, nothing less.'

'Sorry. It's just that seeing you has brought it all back. I can still remember—'

'Harvey!' she snapped. 'Will you stop it? I'm your probation supervisor. We're here to discuss your future, not to reminisce about old times.'

'Flutter,' he said.

'I'm sorry?'

'You used to call me Flutter. Everybody did. They still do.'

'As this relationship is professional, I will address you as Harvey. Is that clear?'

'Whatever you say. You're the boss.'

'Yes, I am,' she said. 'So, let's get down to business, shall we?'

It surprised Flutter to find he fancied her just as much as he had all those years ago, and now an image insinuated itself into his consciousness.

'Oh, I wish,' he muttered.

'I beg your pardon?'

'I said, as you wish,' he lied.

'Good,' she said.

'Can I ask a question?'

'What?'

'Do you remember that day we tried to count the ducks down by the river?'

She sighed in exasperation.

'This really has no relevance to your current situation—'

'Yeah, but do you?' insisted Flutter.

For a moment, it looked as if she was going to lose her temper, then she seemed to relent, and a half-smile flickered on her face.

'I seem to recall you were the one counting,' she said. 'I had more sense than to expect hundreds of ducks to stand still while I counted them.'

'D'you remember how many there were?' asked Flutter.

'No, I don't.'

'237,' he said.

'Only you could remember something as trivial as that,' she said. 'Now, please, can we get back to business?'

'Isn't there a conflict of interest here?'

'Pardon?'

'A conflict of interest. I mean, we were, well, you know...'

'That was years ago, and we were just kids,' she said. 'It isn't the same as two adults.'

'How's that, then? What do adults do that we didn't do? I seem to remember we were pretty adventurous or have I been missing out?'

She was blushing, but he couldn't tell if it was embarrassment or anger.

'It's just different, that's all.'

'It seems the same to me.'

'Well, trust me, it isn't,' she snapped. 'Anyway, I'm a happily married woman now.'

Flutter grinned.

'Ah, so that's why I'm missing out,' he said. 'I'm still single. I didn't realise sex was different for married couples.'

She looked around, clearly embarrassed now.

'Keep your voice down,' she hissed. 'That was a long time ago. The past is the past. It's over and done with!'

Flutter studied her face. She sounded adamant, but he wasn't sure which of them she was trying to convince. He decided it was probably time to stop teasing before she got any more annoyed. Anyway, she was right. It was in the past, and there was no point in dwelling on it, especially if she was going to play the "happily married" card.

'Can I ask another question?'

'Now what?'

'How come you're still in Waterbury? I thought you would have been out exploring the big wide world.'

'I could ask you the same question. Now, can we get on?'

'I have another question.'

She sighed.

'Is it relevant to our professional relationship? If it's not, then the answer is no, you can't.'

'How come you took my case?'

'What makes you think I had a choice?'

'Did you?'

'If you really want to know, we get handed cases, we don't get to choose. But I'll admit when I saw your name, I was curious, and I had a word with my boss and pointed out that, as we had made a mistake, it might make things easier as I knew you.'

'Yeah?' Flutter smiled a smug little smile.

'Don't flatter yourself,' she said. 'It wasn't anything like that. I just wondered how you had sunk so low—'

'I didn't sink so low,' he said. 'I was stitched up.'

'Aren't you supposed to show a degree of contrition?'

'Eh?'

'Contrition. It means—'

'I know what it means, but I'm buggered if I'm going to admit I was in the wrong for doing something I didn't do.'

The atmosphere seemed to have cooled rather rapidly, and she stared at him for what seemed like a very long time, but he didn't back down.

'Okay,' she said, finally, all businesslike. 'Let's get this done, shall we?'

It only took a few minutes for her to run through the rules, Flutter carefully, and deliberately, nodding his head in all the right places.

'Jesus,' he said, eventually. 'All these conditions!'

'This is what happens when you stray from the straight and narrow. Just make sure you remember them, and abide by them, and you'll be fine.'

'I'll do my best, but I might have stopped listening after the first hundred or so.'

'Don't exaggerate. It's not that bad. Anyway, it's your own fault. And don't think because you know me, I'm going to be lenient. I'll probably be tougher.'

'Yeah, that figures.'

'This has got nothing to do with what happened fifteen years ago, and if that's what you think, I suggest you should ask for a different supervisor. You have the right if that's what you want.'

But that was something Flutter definitely didn't want.

'No, you're all right. I'm sure we'll get along just fine.'

'And remember, if you have any problems, I'm always here for you, at the end of the phone. Anytime, day or night. Oh, and I nearly forgot, you're also not allowed a computer or a laptop.'

'I don't have either of those.'

'And no mobile phone.'

'Ah. We might have a problem there.'

'What do you mean?'

'You just said I can call you anytime, day or night. How am I going to do that without a mobile phone?'

Her expression told him she obviously hadn't considered this, so he emphasised his point.

'And before you ask, I don't have a landline, and the nearest call box is miles from my house.'

He sat back and watched her face as she considered what to do.

'What sort of mobile phone is it?' she asked. 'Can I see it?'

Flutter stuck a hand into his pocket.

'It's not one of those smart phones, if that's what you mean,' he said, placing the phone on the table. 'I can't stand them. This one just does calls and texts.'

She looked at the phone.

'It's not really allowed,' she said.

'Take it if you must, but how are you going to be a phone call away if you do?'

'I suppose you have a point,' she said grudgingly.

'And you said I was a special case,' added Flutter with a grin.

'Don't push your luck,' she said. 'I'm going to let you keep the mobile phone for now, but if I find you're using it for anything nefarious...'

'I'm not sure what that means,' said Flutter.

'I think you know exactly what it means.'

'Seriously, I don't.'

Jenny sighed. She knew it was important she stayed professional, but now he was getting under her skin. And that cheeky grin had just the same effect it had all those years ago...

'If you don't know what nefarious means, perhaps you should go to the library, borrow a dictionary, and look it up,' she said. 'And I suggest you stop trying my patience.'

'All right,' he said. 'I'm sorry. You're the boss here, and I'll try to remember that.'

'Good. I hope you do.'

She glanced down at her notes, then gave him an icy smile as she looked up.

'There seems to be some mistake with your paperwork. We seem to have two addresses for you.'

'That's right.'

'I recognised the one in town. Isn't that where you lived with your uncle when we were kids?'

'It's where I grew up. My uncle left it to me.'

'And you also have a house in Willow Grove. Is that correct?'

'That's right. Know it, do you?'

'No, I don't think I do.'

'It's my real dad's house. He died a few months ago and left it to me in his will.'

'That's nice.' She thought for a moment. 'Hang on, I thought your real father died when you were little.'

'Yeah, so did I, but it turns out things weren't quite as I was told. Apparently my uncle thought it would be better if I grew up not knowing the truth, if that makes sense.'

'So, what is the truth?'

'Funnily enough, I've spent the last couple of weeks finding out who my real father was, and what really happened back then.'

She raised an eyebrow.

'Oh, really? So, what is the story?'

Flutter thought telling her he had been associating with gangsters wouldn't work in his favour, even if it hadn't been his choice. Perhaps this would be good to time to be a little economical with the truth.

'It's complicated, but it seems my real dad had another brother, as well as the one who raised me, and that he didn't die years ago, like I was told.'

Jenny looked rather taken aback.

'And this other brother was your real father?'

'You're surprised?' said Flutter. 'How d'you think I feel? It's no wonder I was all mixed up as a kid, is it?'

'You must be sorry you never got to meet him.'

'Not really. I mean, he never gave a damn about me when I needed him, did he? I'm not sure I can forgive him for that.'

'Aren't they big, expensive houses out that way?'

'Oh yeah, it's massive. It's worth a fortune.'

Her interest was obvious now.

'And yet you're living in the small house?'

Flutter nodded.

'It's more like the sort of home I'm used to. Don't forget, I was living in a cell for months. You get used to being cramped up. Big open spaces take a bit of getting used to after that.'

'You know you mustn't move house without letting me know?'

'Yeah, I know. It was rule number one hundred and ninety-something, wasn't it?'

'I'm serious.'

'I'm not planning on moving away from Waterbury. I like it here and I intend to settle here. It's a new start.'

'Even if you move to the bigger house, or go away for just one night, you must tell me.'

'Yeah, yeah. And I must be home by 8 pm, or I'll turn into a pumpkin, and I can't re-emerge until 6 am. It's a bit like being Dracula, but in reverse.'

'I'll have to visit the house to make sure it's suitable.'

'Suitable? You know the house. It's where I grew up. It's where we used to go when we wanted to—'

'Yes. All right, Harvey. I've got the picture. So why don't I check out the house in Willow Grove?'

Flutter wasn't sure this was a good idea. What if Jimmy Jewle turned up while she was there?

'Check it out?'

'Yes. Check the location, see what the neighbours are like, that sort of thing.'

Flutter couldn't help but smile. Jenny obviously did not know about the houses in Willow Grove.

'It's not a bad area,' he said. 'There are one or two dodgy neighbours, but most of them seem okay.'

Her head snapped to attention at the mention of dodgy neighbours, but he held her gaze without flinching.

'I'm not joking. I will come and see it,' she warned, 'and I don't have to call ahead to give you notice.'

'I think it'll be better if you let me know you're coming.'

'Why?'

'Because I don't live there, and there's a security system. You won't be able to get in if I'm not there.'

'I could ask the police to let me in.'

Flutter definitely didn't want the police sniffing around the house.

'I think they've got better things to do than that, don't you? Look, I'm happy to show you around if you really want to see it. Just let me know when and I'll make sure I'm there.'

This seemed to satisfy her for now, and she glanced down at her notes again.

'Have you found a job yet?' she asked.

Flutter wondered what she would make of his current setup with Katie, and once again decided on a little factual economy.

'I've been doing odd jobs for the local newspaper,' he said.

'Doing odd jobs isn't exactly what I meant.'

'It's just temporary at the moment, but it keeps me out of trouble, and it might turn into something permanent. The thing is, I was left some money as well as the house, so I'm not short of readies.'

'I'll need a number so I can speak to someone there,' she said.

'There's just the one lady. She owns and runs the place.'

'Then I need her number.'

'Why?'

'Because I have to make sure it's proper employment, and she's not taking advantage of you.'

'Well, if I'm honest, I wouldn't mind if she did,' said Flutter, 'but, sadly, she's not like that.'

She studied his face again, trying to decide whether to ignore this latest attempt at being a smart-arse, or make a big deal out of it. Flutter gazed innocently back at her.

'Sign here,' she said finally, sliding a sheet of typewritten paper across to him. Without bothering to read a word, Flutter signed and handed it back to her. She slid a blank piece of paper across the table.

'I'd like your newspaper lady's phone number.'

'Her name is Katie Donald,' said Flutter.

'Well, if you write that down with her number, I won't forget it, will I?'

Flutter scribbled Katie's name and number on the sheet of paper and handed it back to her. She slipped it into his folder.

'Our next meeting is on Thursday afternoon, at the same time, but in my office this time. And remember, these meetings are crucial. If ever you think you will miss one, or even be late, you must let me know.'

She handed him a business card.

'Here's my number. As I said, you can call anytime. If I can't answer, leave a message and I'll get back to you.'

'Don't worry, I don't intend to miss any meetings,' he said, slipping the card into his pocket.

'Just make sure you don't.'

She put her head down and began writing notes in his file. As she did, her hair spilled back over her ears and hid her face.

Flutter waited for her to tell him the meeting was over, but she seemed to have forgotten he was there.

'Is that it? Can I go now?' he asked.

'Yes,' she said, without looking up.

Flutter got to his feet.

'Same time on Thursday then, yeah?'

'And don't be late,' she warned.

'I won't. I'm here in Waterbury because I want to make a new start.'

'Remember, I'm here to help you with that, and don't forget to call if you even think you will be late.'

'Yeah, right, got it. I'll do it.'

He walked over to the shop door and opened it but, disappointingly, she didn't look up. As he closed the door and looked down the street, he got the impression he might have seen someone, possibly a woman, running away. He thought there could have have been something vaguely familiar about the runner and, on another day he might have been a bit more curious but, right now, he was too preoccupied to care.

As well as feeling confused and intrigued, Flutter was feeling deflated. It was as if his mission to go straight had just become much harder, and he wondered what the odds were that of all the people who could have been his probation officer, he should end up with the only person he had ever really loved.

Of course, he had been too young to realise it was love when he had been dating her. It was only several years after he had dumped her he understood what a fool he had been, but by then it was much too late to do anything about it. Sadly, this seemed to become the template for Flutter's life and, since then, he had perfected the unfortunate knack of nearly always turning his back on a good thing.

As he wandered away from Leslie's, Flutter wondered about Mr Rodgers and what he was like. Then he wondered why he'd allowed

Jenny to invite herself to inspect the house in Willow Grove. Of course, it was a perfectly reasonable thing for a probation supervisor to want to check out his living arrangements, but he had been so busy trying to be clever she had caught him off guard.

Showing her the house wasn't a problem because it meant he would get to spend more time with her. The real issue was that Jenny had known him when they were teenagers, and she knew how poor his family had been. So, it was inevitable she would want to know more about his real father and where the money had come from to buy such a big house.

If he couldn't come up with a believable story, she might decide to make enquiries through the legal system and if she opened that particular can of worms, who knew where it might end!

CHAPTER 3

At around about the time Flutter had been asking Jenny if she recalled counting the ducks down by the river, Katie was discovering they had run out of coffee back at the office. She didn't like leaving Winston, but he was snoring loudly, and it would only take a few minutes to run down to the shop, grab a takeaway coffee, and run back.

As she approached the shop, she had to walk alongside the shop window and glanced inside. A long narrow mirror ran the width of the room across the back wall. It had been artfully placed at such a height that it made the shop appear much larger than it really was to anyone sitting at a table facing it. It also allowed anyone looking into the shop from Katie's position to see the faces of those with their backs to the window.

She did a double take as she recognised Flutter's face and then instinctively ducked down so he wouldn't see her. Hastily, she took a few paces back, stopped, and then peered cautiously around the edge of the window at the woman sitting across the table from him. Katie guessed she was perhaps just a couple of years older than she herself was, which meant she was closer to Flutter's age.

Her desire for coffee now completely forgotten, Katie observed the couple. There was an obvious attraction between them, which was emphasised by the fact they only had eyes for each other and were oblivious to everyone around them.

Katie felt resentment growing inside her as she wondered who the woman was and why he had lied and told her he was going to see his dentist. If he had a date, why didn't he just say so? It's not as if she cared what he did in his own time, and anyway, it was none of her business. Or was it?

Then she wondered why she had ducked down when she saw him and why she was standing out here in the cold. Why didn't she just walk in and say hello? Lost in these thoughts, she suddenly realised Flutter was walking towards the door. He was looking back at the other woman, and hadn't so much as glanced in her direction yet, but she knew she would have some awkward explaining to do if she stayed where she was when he came through that door. There was only one thing she could do...

Flutter ran up the stairs and pushed through the door into Katie's office. She looked guiltily up from her laptop.

'Are you all right?' he asked.

'Of course. Why do you ask?'

'I dunno. You just look a bit upset. Has Winston been farting again?'

'Winston has been an angel.'

Flutter bent down to take a closer look at her face.

'You look a bit red in the face,' he said with genuine concern. 'And you're sweating. You're not coming down with something, are you?'

He reached out to place the palm of his hand on her forehead, but she angrily swatted the hand away.

'No, I am not coming down with something. It's hot in here, that's all.'

'No, it's not.'

'Well, it is for me today,' she said.

'Why? What's so special about today?'

'Do I have to spell it out?' she snapped.

'There's no need to bite my head off,' said Flutter. 'I'm just looking out for you.'

'Are you going to do this every month?'

Flutter was puzzled.

'Every month? What do you mean every mo—'

As if he was a cartoon character, there was almost an audible clunk as the penny finally dropped for him.

'Oh. I get it. You mean the thing that women... but men don't. Am I right?'

'Oh, well done. Very perceptive,' she said sarcastically. 'We'll make a detective out of you yet.'

Flutter was shocked by her attitude, and took a physical step back to emphasise the point. Then he grabbed Winston's lead.

'Come on, Winston,' he called. 'Time to go home.'

The old dog shambled from his bed beneath Katie's desk and waited patiently while Flutter clipped the lead onto his collar.

'Well, thank you for keeping an eye on him, Katie,' he said, 'but I think it's best if we get out of your way. The atmosphere's a bit toxic in here this afternoon and, for once, it's not Winston's fault.'

'Wait a minute,' said Katie. 'Don't be like that. I didn't mean—'

'Yeah, I'm sure you didn't,' said Flutter, halfway through the door. 'But I didn't mean anything either. I was concerned about you, that's all. I thought it's what friends do, but maybe I got that wrong. Perhaps if I come back in the morning, you'll be in a better mood.'

As he pulled the door closed behind him and disappeared down the stairs, Katie slumped guiltily forward in her chair and slowly lowered her forehead to the desk. Of all the excuses she could have used, why use that one, and then try to make him look small when he didn't immediately get it?

She knew why, of course, she just didn't want to admit it, even to herself!

CHAPTER 4

Tuesday

On Tuesday morning, Flutter and Winston followed what was now their normal routine, entering the park at around 08:30, where Flutter allowed Winston off the leash to explore, and allowed his own mind to wander where it would. It was only after a few minutes of this wandering state that Flutter suddenly became aware Winston was missing. He looked back, expecting him to still be snuffling around the nearest trees, but he wasn't there.

'Winston?'

Alarmed, he turned around and scanned the surrounding area just in time to glimpse the old dog's backside as he headed towards the river. Ahead of the dog, Flutter could just make out a commotion at the water's edge where a couple of people were feeding a vast assortment of ducks and swans.

'Oh, no, not the bird food,' he muttered, as he sprinted after the dog.

As he ran, Flutter wondered how it was possible Winston was always hungry. He'd only been fed half an hour ago, and yet now he was about to barge all the ducks aside and gorge on their food. It was the sort of unfortunate greed that was hard to justify.

Winston had now infiltrated the flock of ducks and appeared to make a beeline for the two older ladies feeding the birds. One lady was in a wheelchair, but it was the other one Winston had recognised and, as he reached her, she appeared to let out an exclamation before bending to fuss over him. As she turned to look for the dog's owner, Flutter knew her immediately. Now he understood the dog's obvious joy, he relaxed, slowing to a walk as she bent to the excited dog once again.

As Flutter approached the bench, he could see the lady feeding the ducks was in a wheelchair, presumably pushed there by the one he knew.

'Hello, Doris,' said Flutter, as he reached the bench. 'Mind if I join you?'

'It's a free country,' she said sniffily. 'I suppose you can sit wherever you want.'

Flutter sat down on the bench. The lady in the wheelchair was totally focused on feeding the birds, seemingly unaware that Flutter and Winston were there.

'How are you?' he asked.

'I've been worse,' she said, cagily. 'I see you're looking after my boy.'

'I do my best,' said Flutter. 'I think he's happy enough, but he obviously misses you.'

'Yes, well, kids and pets are always the ones who suffer most when people have a big falling out.'

'Is that what happened? I thought we had a disagreement, and we just needed to sleep on it overnight.'

'You asked me to leave.'

'No, I didn't. I suggested it would be best if you return to your flat so we could all cool down and not say something we'd regret, that's all. No-one asked you to leave. It was your choice to pack your bags and go marching off in a huff.'

'I wasn't in a huff. You were the one who was angry.'

'I had every right to be angry.'

'I don't see why. I was only trying to help.'

'How was getting us all put away for murder going to help me?'

'The world would be a better place without people like Jimmy Jewle.'

'You're probably right about that, but that's not really the point, is it?'

'Well, what is the point? You never explained why you were so angry.'

'I seem to recall I made it pretty clear at the time, but if you can't remember, I'll tell you again. Having a gangster turn up at my gate demanding I give him my house isn't something I have to deal with every day and, as if that wasn't stressful enough, you then marched down the drive and pointed a shotgun at him!'

'It's the only language people like him understand. It made him go away, didn't it?'

'For a few hours, yes. But now I know he's there, in the background, like a gigantic black shadow, just waiting to screw things up for me whenever it suits him.'

'Well, he wouldn't be if you'd let me pull the trigger. I would have been more than happy to do it.'

'Yes, I'm sure you would, but then I would have been an accessory to murder.'

'That's the bit I don't understand. I would have been the one who pulled the trigger.'

'Yeah, but I was standing there next to you. I'd only been out of prison for five minutes. With my family history, do you really think anyone would believe I wasn't somehow responsible? Before you know it, I would have been locked away for another crime I didn't commit.'

Doris sighed. She still couldn't see it, but she thought Flutter probably knew more about these things. Besides, she was tired of arguing, and she had been missing Winston. She bent down to fuss with the old dog.

Flutter didn't see any point in continuing the argument either.

What had happened was in the past and couldn't be changed. Doris hadn't pulled the trigger, and no-one had died so, what did it matter? Besides, Winston was ecstatic at seeing Doris again, and he didn't want to spoil that.

'I thought you must have moved away from Waterbury, as I hadn't seen you around,' said Flutter.

'And where would I go?' said Doris. 'I've been living like a recluse for years. I lost contact with everyone I used to know.'

'Where are you living?'

Doris nodded towards the lady in the wheelchair.

'With Alma. She's my aunt, the only family I've got left, and the only person I kept in touch with. I persuaded her to move down here a few years ago so I could keep an eye on her. I'm staying in her spare room.'

'I tried to give Jewle the house, but he wants me to keep it,' said Flutter.

'That doesn't sound like him,' said Doris. 'What's the catch?'

'The catch is he thinks he owns me and he can call on me whenever he wants. That's what I meant about him lurking in the background.'

'So, what are you going to do?'

'I told him I don't want the house and he can have it.'

'Ouch. That must hurt.'

'It's not so bad. I didn't really feel right in that great big house, and the neighbours didn't exactly make me feel welcome. And the way I see it, if I give him the house, he can't use it as leverage against me.'

Doris nodded her approval of his logic.

'So, where are you going to live?'

'My uncle left me a house, too. It's only a little terraced house, and it needs a bit of work, but at least it's mine and there are no strings attached.'

'Well, good for you. I hope it all works out and you get Jewle off your back. How's it going with that girl?'

'You mean, Katie? I thought you didn't like her.'

'It doesn't matter what I like. She's your girlfriend.'

Flutter smiled.

'Actually, you're wrong. It's not like that. We're just friends, and we work together.'

'You mean your detective agency?'

'You heard about it?'

'I read the story in the local paper. Is it working out?'

'Its early days yet,' said Flutter. 'That's where I'm going now, actually.'

'But have you got any work?'

'To be honest, no, we haven't, but there's plenty of time.'

'It sounds a bit pie in the sky, if you ask me,' said Doris. 'I can't see much call for one private eye in such a small town, never mind two of you.'

'Yeah, well, maybe you're right, but there aren't many jobs to choose from when you're an ex-con like me. And if it doesn't work out, I'll just have to find something else.'

Alma, the lady in the wheelchair, finally exhausted her supply of bread, and shook the final few crumbs from the bag, provoking a mad scramble of ducks around her feet. She folded the bag neatly in half, and in half again, tucked it into her coat pocket, and then turned to look at Flutter.

'Is this the boy, Harvey?' she asked Doris.

Flutter smiled.

'That's me,' he said. 'Although most people call me Flutter.'

'Has Doris told you?'

Flutter turned to Doris, puzzled.

'Told me what?'

'It's a long story,' said Doris.

Flutter looked at his watch.

'Give me a short version.'

'Alma can do that better than me,' said Doris.

Flutter gave Alma his full attention.

'I didn't get round to reading last week's local newspaper until last night,' she said. 'Inside there's a notice saying an old friend of mine is being buried on Thursday of next week.'

'Oh, I'm sorry,' said Flutter. 'Was it a close friend?'

Alma smiled a sad little smile.

'Reggie Fulshaw. He was my boyfriend when I was sixteen. Then he went off to Malaysia to do his National Service, and I never saw him again.'

'He didn't come back?'

'Oh yes, he came back.'

'So where's he been all this time? Was he living locally? Did you try to get in touch with him?'

'Oh no. I couldn't possibly have done that. He came back in a wooden box.'

Flutter didn't immediately realise what she had said.

'I'm sorry?'

'He died out there in 1960.'

'But I thought you said he was being buried next week!'

'That's what it says in the paper. 11:00, Thursday morning, next week.'

She handed him a copy of the newspaper folded to reveal the funeral notice.

Flutter read the notice.

'I'm confused,' he said. 'If he's being buried next Thursday, and he died in 1960, where's his body been all this time?'

'That's what I want to know,' said Alma, 'because there's been a grave in the cemetery bearing his name since 1960.'

'Did you attend that funeral?'

'In 1960? No, I didn't, but then I didn't know he was dead. If he was,' she added mysteriously.

'What d'you mean, "if he was"?'

'Well, maybe that's not really his grave in the cemetery. Perhaps he's been alive all this time. But if he's not in there, who is?'

'I see what you mean,' said Flutter. 'It's a strange one, isn't it?'

'Everything about it's strange if you ask me. I only found out the grave was there by accident, and that was five years after they had buried him.'

'How come?'

'Someone placed one of those "In Memoriam" notices in the local newspaper. It said it was to mark the fifth anniversary of his death. When I first saw it, I couldn't believe it was true, so I went down to the cemetery and searched among the graves. It took me ages, but I finally found him. Stuck right in a corner, he was.'

'It sounds like you think they had hidden him,' suggested Flutter.

'Why else would they tuck him away in a corner? They didn't even give him a proper headstone, just a tatty old bit of wood.'

'So you think, if he really died in 1960, someone buried him in secret?'

'If he died in action in Malaysia, that would have been worthy of a decent burial, wouldn't it?' asked Alma.

'I don't know much about these things, but you would think so, wouldn't you?' agreed Flutter.

'He used to write to me, you know. When the letters stopped coming, I assumed he'd gone off me. Then five years later I found out he was dead!'

She stopped for a moment, upset at the memory. Flutter kept quiet and gave her time to regain her composure.

'I was so upset to think he had gone and I had missed my chance to say goodbye,' she said wistfully, and now a tear made its way slowly down her cheek.

Flutter put a comforting hand on her shoulder.

'I'm going to be late for work, but I know someone who works for the newspaper. Let me see if I can find out what's going on,' he suggested gently.

'D'you think you could?'

'I can't promise I'll learn anything, but I can promise I'll try,' he said.

As Flutter stood up from the bench, Doris stood with him and walked a few steps with him.

'You're not just saying it. You will try to help, won't you?'

'Of course I will. It's not as if I'm rushed off my feet right now.'

'I phoned the vicar to see what I could find out. I thought he might be able to put Alma's mind at rest, but he knew nothing about it. He says there is no funeral next Thursday, so now I don't know what to think.'

'There's no denying it sounds weird.'

'I thought you'd say something like that. We haven't got much money, and I really don't like to ask, but please help us. She was so upset by it, and she's not got long to live, you see.'

Flutter glanced back at Alma, but she was staring off into the distance, reliving a long forgotten memory.

'Oh, Doris, that's terrible. I'm so sorry.'

'It's always bothered her about Reggie, and I'd like her to know what really happened to him before she goes.'

'And the name is Reggie Fulshaw. Have I got that right?'

'That's it,' said Doris. 'There is one more thing. Can I see Winston now and then?'

'I don't see why not. I think he'd love it. Let me text you my new number and you can send me your address. When I come to let you know what I've found out, I'll bring him with me, if that's okay.'

'Yes, I'd like that, and so would Alma.'

CHAPTER 5

'Morning, Katie,' said Flutter. 'Sorry I'm late. I got a bit held up.'

'There's no need to apologise. In fact, if anyone should apologise, it's me.'

'Why's that?'

'As if you didn't know. I'm talking about yesterday afternoon when I bit your head off. There was no need for me to behave like that.'

'Don't worry about it,' said Flutter. 'I won't hold it against you. Anyway, I've made a note on my calendar, so I'll be on my guard next time.'

Katy was horrified.

'You've done what?'

He gave her his best cheeky grin.

'I haven't, really. I'm kidding. But trust me, you don't need to apologise. We all have bad days now and then.'

'Can I ask why you're looking so pleased with yourself? Or is it simply because I've apologised?'

'I've just seen Doris.'

'Doris?' echoed Katie.

'Yeah, you know, Doris, the housekeeper that was.'

'Yes, I remember who Doris is. I'm just wondering, after what nearly happened, if that's something you should be pleased about.'

'Look, she meant well, and no-one died, did they?'

'Well, you've certainly changed your tune!'

'Yeah, well, I've decided I don't want to spend my life keeping track of grudges. If I'm going to hold a grudge in the future, it's got to be for a good reason.'

Katie had a retort ready, but kept it to herself. She'd had words over the weekend with her on-off boyfriend, Robbie Bright, and she really didn't want more of the same with Flutter.

'So, why are you so pleased at meeting Doris?'

'Because she asked me for a favour, and she misses Winston, so, I'm hoping if I can do the favour, she'll return it by agreeing to babysit him now and then.'

'What is this favour?' asked Katie. 'And why do I feel it involves me?'

'It was Winston who found Doris. She was down by the river with her aunty, feeding the ducks. I've never seen so many ducks. They were everywhere.'

'Does aunty have a name?'

'Alma something. I didn't get her surname.'

'Ah! That explains the ducks,' said Katie. 'Alma is a local legend. They call her the Duck Lady. She's been feeding the ducks for years. The ducks even learned which bus she came in on and used to come to the stop and wait for it to arrive. Then traffic would be brought to a standstill as they swarmed across the road to meet her.'

'Ha! I bet that went down well,' said Flutter.

'It was worse than you think. She used to come in on the 08:15 bus. I know this is only a small town, but even small towns have a rush hour. Can you imagine all those people trying to drive to work and take their kids to school suddenly faced with a road full of ducks?'

'What happened? Did they stop her feeding the ducks?'

'It didn't come to that. The police persuaded her to get a different bus and get off on the other side of the park, away from the town centre. The ducks soon worked it out. Within a week, they were gathering on the other side of the park and traffic got back to normal. But I heard she stopped coming in on the bus to feed them a few weeks ago.'

'I think you'll find that's because she's a very sick lady and she can't get around like she used to. Doris is looking after her now, and takes her to the river in a wheelchair. She says Alma's not got long to live.'

'That's a shame. I never really knew her, but I used to see her around and I knew the legend. She was a one-off if ever there was one.'

'Yeah, well, really, she's the one who needs the favour, not Doris.'

'So, what is this favour?'

'It's a bit of a love story actually, or perhaps a "love lost" story.'

He couldn't tell from her expression if she was interested or not, but then she spoke.

'Go on, then. Tell me more.'

'There's a funeral notice in the local paper.' he said. 'Alma says the man whose supposed to be getting buried already has a grave in the cemetery.'

A wry smile crossed her face.

'Perhaps Alma made a mistake.'

'You think so?' asked Flutter. 'Only Doris called the vicar to check, and he told her there is no funeral booked for any day next week.'

'Ah,' was all she could say. 'I'll see if I can find out who placed the notice.'

'Doris thinks there's something funny going on, and I agree with her,' said Flutter.

'Why would Doris think that?'

'Well, apart from the non-funeral, the man in question was Alma's boyfriend. She says they buried him in secret in 1960.'

'They buried him in secret? Who are they?'

'That's what she wants to know. She didn't even know the guy was dead until someone posted one of those "In Memoriam" notices five years later. Since then, the same notice has appeared every year. Don't you think that's odd?'

She pulled a face.

'I expect his family misses him. It's not unusual.'

'The thing is, he didn't have any family. He was an orphan.'

He could see he had her full attention now.

'And now there's notice of a second funeral, which the vicar says isn't happening,' she muttered.

'Doesn't it make you wonder what's going on?'

'You really want to do this, don't you?' asked Katie.

'Don't you?'

'Does Alma have any money to pay us?'

'I don't think she's got much.'

'We can't afford to work for nothing. We're not a charity.'

'I know you've got your job but, unlike you, I've got nothing better to do, so I thought it wouldn't hurt if I looked through the newspaper archive. You do have an archive, right?'

'Of course I have an archive but, if I'm honest, I have nothing better to do, either,' said Katie. 'I really don't think I can carry on with the newspaper anymore. Even online, hardly anyone reads it. I'm losing money hand over fist.'

'You've still got Jewle's cheque,' said Flutter. 'You could cash it.'

'Over my dead body,' said Katie. 'I wouldn't take money from that man if he was my last resort.'

'I don't want to sound clever, but it sounds like he is your last resort, and you earned it fair and square.'

'We're not having this conversation now, and I want you to promise you won't mention it again.'

Flutter was well aware of Katie's feelings about Jimmy Jewle, but he was also aware Katie hadn't actually destroyed the cheque. He almost said as much, but then realised what the consequences of such a foolish action might be, and thought better of it.

'Okay, fair enough,' he said. 'I promise I'll try not to mention it again.'

'Good.'

'So, what do you want to do about Alma?'

'I think we should speak to her.'

'What now?'

'There's no time like the present, is there?'

'But I don't know where she lives.'

'Then it's just as well I do know.'

'You do? How come?'

'I'm a journalist, remember?'

'I think we should let them know we're coming.'

'You've got Doris's number, haven't you?'

'Oh, yeah. You're right, I have. I'll call her. What time do you want to go?'

'Whatever time suits Alma. It's not far, we can walk it in ten minutes.'

Half an hour later, when they got to Alma's house, Flutter handed Winston's lead to Doris.

'There you go,' he said. 'I told you I'd bring him. You can keep him for the rest of the day if you like.'

'Really? You don't mind? That would be wonderful.'

'He'll love all the attention,' said Flutter. 'It'll be a change from sleeping all day. I'll collect him on my way home.'

'I'll take him in the other room while you speak to Alma. She's through there.'

She pointed them through to a small, neat, sitting room and took Winston off to the kitchen.

'Alma, this is my friend Katie who works at the local paper,' said Flutter. 'I told her your story, and she'd like to help you.'

'Hello Alma,' said Katie. 'I'll do my best to help but I need I'm going to need a little background first. So, can I ask you a few questions?'

'Of course,' said Alma.

'So, your friend Reggie was a local lad?' asked Katie.

'He was an orphan,' said Alma. 'There used to be a small orphanage on the edge of town. He lived there.'

'How did you meet him?'

'A travelling funfair used to come to town every year. I went with my friend one Saturday afternoon so she could meet her boyfriend without her parents knowing. I didn't want to play gooseberry, so after she met him, I wandered off on my own.

'And that's when this lovely boy called Reggie came along and started talking to me. We spent the entire afternoon together, and then he walked me home. Ever so polite he was, but I knew my dad wouldn't approve, so I made him leave me at the end of our road.'

'And you carried on seeing him?'

'Oh yes. We went to the cinema a few times, but then he got called up to do his National Service. They all had to do it back then. Just eighteen years old he was when he went off to do his basic training.'

'Did you keep in touch?'

'We exchanged letters, but I was never sure if he was just being polite, you know? The words seemed to be rather stiff, formal almost, as if perhaps his heart wasn't really in it. Then one day he came to see me unexpectedly. He told me he was being posted to Malaya, or Malaysia, as it is now, for a year. He said I shouldn't worry as he wouldn't come to any harm because they were going to a safe area, and we'd get together again when he came back.'

'What happened after he went away? Did he keep on writing?'

'Yes, he did.'

'In that case, he must have been keen on you,' said Katie. 'Going abroad would have been the perfect excuse to stop writing.'

'I suppose you're right, but I only had five or six more letters, then I never heard from him again. Heartbreaking, it was. I thought he'd ended it, but didn't want to tell me. Then five years later I saw this notice in the newspaper...'

Flutter noticed her eyes glistening, and he felt a pang of guilt, although why he should feel guilty, he did not understand.

'I'm sorry, Alma,' he said, softly. 'It must have been difficult to accept, especially with you both being so young.'

'Difficult to accept?' she repeated. 'You can say that again. It didn't seem right back then, and it still doesn't seem right now.'

'I must admit, it makes you wonder what happened,' said Katie.

'Yes, doesn't it?' said Alma wistfully.

'It's possible he did something that brought disgrace to the Army. They're funny about stuff like that.'

'I can't see it,' said Alma. 'Reggie was one of those people who always tried to do the right thing. I'm sure he wouldn't have broken any rules. It would be nice to know the truth, though.'

For a moment she stared off at nothing, as if remembering the past. Then she was suddenly back with them again.

'Do you think you can find out what happened?'

'After all this time, I'm not sure,' said Katie, 'but it won't hurt to dig around and see what we can find out.'

'That's very kind of you.'

Flutter looked deliberately at his watch. He had agreed with Katie beforehand that they wouldn't stay long at this first meeting.

'I suppose we ought to get going,' he said.

'Hold on a minute,' said Alma. 'I've got something for you.'

She produced a small bundle of letters bound with a faded red ribbon.

'It took me a while to find them,' she said, 'but I knew I had them somewhere.'

She offered the bundle to Katie.

'What's this?' she asked.

'It's some letters Reggie sent me.'

'You've kept them all this time?'

'I seem to have lost some of the earliest ones from before he went abroad, but these are all the ones from Malaysia. He was the only one who ever sent me love letters, so I suppose that made them even more special to me,' she said proudly. 'I've never shown them to anyone before.'

'Are you sure you want us to have them? They're obviously precious to you.'

'I know you'll look after them for me,' she said. 'And there might be stuff in there that will help you find out what happened.'

Katie carefully took the bundle of letters and passed them to Flutter, who slipped them into his pocket.

'We'll get to work as soon as we get back to the office,' promised Katie.

'Is there something you'd like to tell me?' asked Katie as they began walking away from Alma's house.

'I don't think so,' said Flutter.

Katie turned her head to look at him as they walked.

'Are you sure?'

Flutter looked at Katie. She had a determined look about her, and he wondered what this was about.

'I had a phone call first thing this morning,' she said. 'From someone claiming to be your probation supervisor.'

'Ah! Right. Yeah, about that. I was going to tell you.'

'Well, she beat you to it.'

'Sorry. I was waiting for the right moment to tell you.'

'I've known you for several weeks now and you've never mentioned it,' she said. 'Do you think the right moment would ever have arrived if she hadn't called?'

'What? No, no, it's not like that. I only found out myself on Monday.'

'On Monday? You mean yesterday? You're joking!'

'It's no joke, Katie. I'm dead serious. I got a letter yesterday telling me I was on probation. It was the first I knew about it.'

'Isn't that sort of thing usually arranged before you're released?'

'Apparently there was some sort of admin cock-up and I was missed.'

'That sounds unlikely.'

'Unlikely, or not, it's happened,' said Flutter.

'It sounds fishy if you ask me,' said Katie. 'Anyway, why didn't you just tell me?'

'I was going to, but it's not something I want to brag about, is it? I wanted to find out how it would affect me before I told you.'

'It would have been a lot easier to handle her phone call if I'd been expecting it.'

'You didn't tell her about us being detectives, did you?'

'Of course not.'

'Blimey. You didn't lie to her, did you, Katie?'

'She didn't specifically ask about being a detective, so I didn't specifically tell her that's what we were hoping to do.'

'Oh, right. I suppose that's fair enough, then. The thing is, I couldn't lie when she asked me about a job, but I didn't think she'd check up so soon. I would have told you if I'd thought she'd check me out that fast.'

'So, what did you tell her?'

'That I was doing odd jobs for the local newspaper and that it might become a permanent position. I didn't go into detail about what exactly the odd jobs were.'

'Well, lucky for you, she told me what you'd said and asked me if it was true. If she'd asked me first, I might have told her about starting up a detective agency. Can you be a detective if you're on probation?'

'I dunno. Maybe I'll ask at our next meeting.'

As they walked on, it occurred to Katie that perhaps this was the woman she saw Flutter with in Leslie's coffee shop. But then, when she remembered the way they were looking at each other, she thought surely not. She really wanted to ask, but if she did, would he think she had been spying on him?

'She seemed to be rather possessive of you when I spoke to her,' she said, finally.

'She's worried you're going to take advantage of me.'

'Sleeping with the boss is not part of the deal.'

'Not like that. She thinks you will pay me naff all, and make me work 24/7.'

'Why would she think that?'

'She would rather see me with a career.'

'D'you think she's going to stop you working with me?'

'Who knows? I told her I don't need a career because I have an allowance. I'm sure she disapproves, but she couldn't really argue with me.'

'When's this next meeting? I want to make sure you don't miss it.'

'Thursday afternoon.'

'Right. Now I know, I'll make sure you're there.'

CHAPTER 6

WHEN THEY GOT BACK to the office, it took Katie less than ten minutes to check the funeral notice that had been placed in her newspaper.

'I'm afraid this funeral notice won't be much help,' she said. 'It's handwritten and was posted through the letterbox. Cash payment enclosed.'

'Is there a name?' asked Flutter.

'Smith.'

Flutter's heart sank.

'Is there an address?'

'It's the shop downstairs,' said Katie, 'but I can tell you there's no-one called Smith works down there and if they've had a bereavement, they don't seem to be bothered about it.'

'Don't you check these things when they come in?' asked Flutter, trying not to show his irritation.

'I rarely feel the need with funeral notifications,' she said, adding defiantly, 'I'm sorry I'm not perfect. It's what comes from running on a shoestring.'

Flutter felt suitably chastened.

'Sorry,' he said. 'That was out of order. I was just—'

'—hoping for a simple answer?' she asked with a smile. 'It wouldn't be much of a conundrum if you could solve it that easily, would it?'

'I suppose if they posted it through your letterbox, it suggests we're looking for someone local. What about the In Memoriam notices? Any luck there?'

'Hang on. I'm just checking that.'

The PC that was used to run the newspaper lived under her desk. It was an ancient machine that hadn't been updated in years as Katie didn't see the point in spending any more than she had to on a failing operation. Flutter hadn't noticed it before because she mostly used a laptop, but now as she lifted the cover that hid the monitor it whirred and buzzed as it came to life.

'Jesus, what's that old thing?' he asked.

'It's called a PC. We thought it was the best thing since sliced bread when we first got it.'

'Is it the one they had on Noah's ark?'

Katie smiled.

'You can laugh. It might be old, but it does the job, albeit rather slowly.'

She typed her query, prodded "enter" and sat back to wait. The computer buzzed and whirred even more, and the green text on the grey screen seemed to go brighter. Then the huge box-like monitor went blank.

Flutter sighed.

'Is it supposed to do that?'

'Probably not,' she said, 'but don't worry, it always happens when you ask it to do a search. Just give it a minute and it'll come back to life.'

Sure enough, after a minute, the screen slowly began to glow again.

'See, I said it would,' she said, studying the screen. 'Oh, that's weird.'

'What?'

'It says they booked it in 1965 and paid a fee, ad infinitum.'

'What does that mean?'

'Basically, the notice will be placed every year forever. My Dad was running this place then. He must have done a deal on the price.'

'So who booked it?' asked Flutter.

'No idea,' she said. 'Anything from that far back won't be in the computer archive.'

Flutter sighed.

'So we're no further forward.'

'If you don't mind me saying, you give up far too easily,' said Katie.

'What's that supposed to mean? If you don't have the records, then we've got nothing.'

'I didn't say I don't have the records. All I said was it's not on the computer, but that's not the end of the world. We have a paper archive.'

'What? Going back that far?'

'I can't promise it will be there, but we can always have a look.'

It was obvious Flutter wasn't keen.

'Unless,' she prompted, 'you'd rather give up and tell your friend it was too much trouble.'

'No way! I'm not giving up that easily.'

'Good, I should hope not. But I think we should read through the letters first in case there's something else that needs checking in the archive,' said Katie.

'That sounds like a plan,' said Flutter.

'I've got about an hour's work I need to do first. So, I suggest you read through the letters, and when I've finished, I'll do the same. Then we can compare notes.'

Flutter eased the precious bundle from his pocket and set it down on the left side of his desk, patting the letters as if to reassure them they were in expert hands. He made himself and Katie a cup of tea, found an unused notebook and pencil, and settled in his chair.

Then he carefully untied the ribbon around the bundle and set it to one side. Now he could see there were ten letters in total. Taking the first letter from the top of the pile, he solemnly placed it on the desk in front of him and carefully examined both sides. Then he opened the envelope, removed the letter from inside, and unfolded it.

He stared at the letter for a few seconds, then compared it to the envelope. It was immediately obvious they were written with different hands. He made a mental note to compare the others as he went through them and, not sure if it was important or not, he made a note in his book. Then he began to read.

It was clear from the first letter that the writer wasn't the most articulate young man, but it was equally obvious he considered Alma to be the best thing that had ever happened to him. Flutter thought this was hardly surprising if the poor guy had grown up in an orphanage sixty years ago. He knew little about orphanages back then, but he knew they weren't known for being havens of warmth and tenderness.

Over the next hour, he read through the first six letters, making occasional notes and re-reading each of them two or three times, to ensure he missed nothing. In each case, he noted the difference in writing between envelope and letter, and although it appeared the same person had written all the letters, another had written all the envelopes. It was at this point that Katie finished her work and started on the letters.

There was no mention of being posted abroad until the fourth letter. The remaining letters told how much Reggie was missing Alma, and how the chaplain had realised he was lonely and taken him under his wing, but they offered precious little information regarding Malaysia. At first, Flutter thought this was a little odd, but then it occurred to him such references were probably excluded to avoid being censored.

Despite what Alma had said about the letters, Flutter thought it was blindingly obvious Reggie idolised his girlfriend, and while he didn't say so in as many words, reading between the lines, there was every sign he intended to see her again just as soon as he returned. As Flutter placed the ninth letter down on the right side of his desk, he glanced at his notebook and sighed. There was so little to go on, he had barely filled two pages.

He reached for the last letter and immediately felt a little wave of optimism. This one felt a little fatter, and firmer, than the others. As he brought it across, he studied the name and address as he had all the others. He often thought his own hand-written scrawl looked as if a demented spider had been break-dancing across the page, but the writing he saw on this envelope was so elegant he felt a twinge of envy!

He was about to open the envelope when something made him look at it again. He felt he was missing something obvious, but he didn't realise what it was until he picked up one of the other envelopes and compared them. Now it was obvious; the writing on this envelope was from a different hand again.

Not sure if it meant anything or not, he made a note in his book, then took out the letter. As he did, a faded sepia photograph dropped into his lap. He picked up the photo and studied it. Three young men dressed in football kit smiled back at him. He turned the photo over. On the back, it looked as if a four-year-old with poor writing skills had printed the footballers' names, and a few other words.

The ink had faded over time, and it took Flutter a few minutes to decipher the words, but finally, he was sure. It read:

BILLY RIGHT HALF REGGIE CENTRE HALF ERNIE LEFT HALF. COMPANY FOOTBALL TEAM 1960

The terms were distinctly old-fashioned, but Flutter knew they referred to the positions the three lads had played in the football team.

He flipped the photo over and wondered which lad was which, and made a note to show the photograph to Alma and see if she could identify them. At least she could tell him which one was Reggie. That would be a start.

He spent another half hour reading the letter, and going through his notes again, then stood from his chair to stretch his weariness away. He passed the photograph to Katie as he made his way to the kitchen to make another cup of tea. But as he waited for the kettle to boil the photograph of the three lads, and the thought that one of them would be dead within months of the photograph being taken haunted him. It didn't seem right. They all looked so young...

'So, what d'you think?' he asked as he placed a mug of tea on her desk.

'I think Alma was very lucky. This guy adored her. It's so romantic. I can't imagine anyone I've ever known writing to me like that.'

'That wasn't quite what I meant.'

She smiled.

'Yes, I know, but it's true. They were much more romantic times.'

'Don't you think the language is sort of basic?' he asked.

'You said he was an orphan, so he was hardly likely to have gone to the best schools, was he? That would suggest he was perhaps not as articulate as you and I. He sounds like he was a good hard-working man, but maybe not the sharpest knife in the box.'

'I wondered if maybe he couldn't read or write,' suggested Flutter. 'Perhaps he dictated and someone else, maybe one of the other lads in the photograph, wrote the letters for him.'

'That wouldn't be unheard of,' she agreed, 'and it goes hand in hand with not being very articulate. It could also explain why there's different writing on the envelopes and letters.'

Flutter tapped the photograph.

'If these three were close mates, maybe one wrote the letters, and one wrote the envelopes, all except the tenth letter.'

'That one intrigues you, doesn't it?' she asked, pointing at the last letter.

'Yeah, it does. Like you said, all the other letters and envelopes are in the same unfussy style, but then the envelope for letter number ten, the last one he ever sent, is from a much more educated hand.'

She looked at the envelope.

'Yes, you're right. The first nine are by the hands of a worker, but the tenth is from the hand of an artist. So, what does it mean?'

'I haven't got a clue,' said Flutter.

She laughed.

'Me neither, but it's a curiosity, that's for sure. What about the football photo? How do we know which one is which?'

'Well, logic says they would stand in their team positions,' said Flutter, 'but we can't be sure, so I thought I'd take the photo with me and ask Alma when I go to collect Winston.'

'Good idea,' said Katie.

'But it's a bit early to be going home, so how about you show me the archive?' suggested Flutter.

'I'm sorry?'

'The archive. I thought I could start going through it now.'

Katie smiled.

'Ah, yes, about that. You understand anything, and everything, that happened before computers is on paper, not on a hard disk.'

Flutter wasn't following.

'Yeah, right. So?'

'So, we're talking about a weekly newspaper that's been going for almost a hundred years.'

Flutter looked around the room.

'You wouldn't fit a fraction of it in here,' said Katie.

Reality was slowly dawning on Flutter.

'So, where is it?'

'The complete archive is stored in a warehouse not far from here, but it would be better if we both go. And I warn you, it's been stored there for years, so it's very dusty. You'll need to wear some sort of overall or your very oldest clothes.'

'Crap!' said Flutter.

'Of course, if you'd rather not bother...'

'No, it's fine, I'll do it,' said Flutter. 'I'm not worried about a bit of dust. When do you want to start?'

'I'm out all day tomorrow, so how about Thursday morning?'

'You're on,' said Flutter.

'Well, there's not much more we can do here,' said Katie. 'You might as well go home.'

'Right. I'll fetch Winston, and I'll see you on Thursday morning.'

'That's Reggie in the middle,' said Alma, pointing at the photograph. 'Not that you'd know it with his hair all cut short like that. He used to have lovely ginger curls, and the most striking blue eyes. He was pretty for a boy, don't you think? And when he smiled, well…'

'He adored you,' said Flutter.

Alma smiled coyly.

'D'you think so?' she asked.

'You've read the letters,' said Flutter. 'You know very well it's so. Like you said, the writing's a bit basic, but there's no doubt how he felt about you.'

Now Alma sighed and gazed sadly off at some distant memory.

'Yes. I often wonder what might have been,' she said. 'My husband was a good man, and we had a good life, but I couldn't help but wonder, especially after he died and I was left on my own.'

Flutter didn't quite know how to respond, and was feeling a little uncomfortable, but Alma was quick to rescue him.

'Listen to me getting all maudlin about something I can't change,' she said. 'That's what old age does to you sometimes.'

When she had told him about Reggie that morning, Flutter had worked out Alma must be in her late seventies.

'I always think it's state of mind, luv,' he said. 'You're only old when you think you are.'

She smiled fondly.

'A state of mind? I wish it was that simple. If it was, I'd think myself dead, and get it over with.'

Flutter was now feeling distinctly out of his depth with the way the conversation was heading, but as if she understood, Alma came to his rescue and changed the subject.

'Were those letters any help?'

'We've been studying them all afternoon, but, to be honest, there's not a great deal to go on. D'you want them back?'

Flutter had brought the letters with him.

'No, you can keep them for now,' she said. 'You might need to refer to them again. I found something else he gave me before he went away. I've got it here.'

She produced a small box, carefully slipped the lid off, peeled back some layers of tissue paper, gazed longingly at the contents, then handed it to him.

Flutter took the box with exaggerated care and gazed down at the contents.

'It's a cap badge, isn't it?'

Alma nodded.

'Yes. I'm sure he would have got into trouble giving it to me, but he didn't seem to care about that. He just wanted me to have something as a keepsake. Is it any help?'

'I'm not sure. If nothing else, it tells us which regiment he was in.'

'Are you going to start there?'

'We thought we'd try the newspaper archive first,' he said. 'We're hoping we can find some news from the time that might help, and find out who asked for the funeral notice to be printed.'

As he collected Winston, Flutter asked Doris if she would have Winston again on Thursday morning.

'It's only for the day, but Katie says the archive is full of dust, and I'm sure breathing it in won't do him any good,' he explained.

'We'd love to have him,' said Doris. 'He's no trouble and Alma enjoys having him around. We'll be down by the river again. Why don't you meet us there?'

'Thanks Doris. That would be great.'

'As we're doing each other all these favours, can I ask one more?'

'Of course you can,' said Flutter.

'I know you don't live there anymore, but do you still have access to the big house in Willow Grove?'

'Yes, I do.'

'I left some of my stuff in the flat above the garage. Can I come and collect it some time?'

'Of course you can,' said Flutter. 'Give me a week or so and I'll arrange a free afternoon and ask Katie if I can borrow her car.'

CHAPTER 7

Thursday

'Are you telling me those are old clothes?' asked Katie when he got to the office. 'They'll get ruined. I told you not to wear good stuff.'

Flutter was carrying a rucksack, which he now raised for her to see.

'Don't worry,' he said. 'I've got two paper overalls I got from the DIY store when I was decorating my house. There's one each in here.'

'Oh,' said Katie. 'If I'd known you had those, I wouldn't have worn these old rags. I feel distinctly under-dressed now.'

'Will there be judges?' asked Flutter.

'Of course not.'

'Stop worrying, then. You look fine. Besides, once we get them on, we'll both look like Smurfs, so who cares?'

'Smurfs?'

'Didn't I say? The suits are blue. Sorry about that, but at least they'll keep us clean. Anyway, no-one is going to see you except me, and I'm going to look the same.'

This seemed to appease Katie momentarily, but now something else was bothering her.

'Where's Winston?'

'I thought he'd probably get in the way, so Doris is babysitting him.'

'Are you sure you can trust her with him?'

'I know you don't like her, but don't forget she was looking after him before I came along. He's quite safe, and he knows her. It works for both of them.'

'I suppose you're right.'

'Of course I am.'

'Did Alma identify Reggie and his mates?'

'Yeah, she did. I wrote it down from left to right so we won't forget whose who. And she gave me something else...'

He removed the small box from the rucksack and handed it to her.

Carefully, she prised the lid from the box and removed the badge.

'It's a Royal Hampshire Regiment cap badge,' she said.

'You know it?' asked Flutter.

'I have a great-uncle who spent half his life as part of it.'

'Well, that'll save me some time. I thought I might look them up.'

'Well, good luck with that. The Regiment doesn't exist anymore. They were amalgamated with a few other regiments, years ago, to save money.'

'Damn. I was hoping I could get some information from them.'

She gave him a pitying look.

'You've got a lot to learn, haven't you?'

'How d'you mean?'

'The Army isn't in the habit of sharing information with anyone, no matter who they are. And that's especially the case when they have something to hide.'

'D'you think they have?'

'That's what we're going to find out, isn't it?'

'Yes, it is, so let's get started. Where's this archive of yours?'

'We'll have to drive there. My car's down in the car park.'

Flutter followed her down to the car park and over to her car. He had been awake half the night worrying what Katie really thought about him being on probation. Did she feel it was an obstacle to them working together? Perhaps if he raised the subject with a bit of subtlety, he might find out.

'Don't forget I need to be back by three-thirty,' he said.

'Oh yes, for that hot date with your probation supervisor.'

'Ha, ha, hilarious.'

'I take it you can drive?' she asked.

Flutter took this change in the direction of the conversation as a sign Katie wasn't losing sleep over his situation. Perhaps he was worrying unnecessarily.

'Of course I can drive,' he said.

'D'you want to drive now?'

'What? In you car?'

'That's what I was thinking.'

'Are you sure?'

Katie looked from the old car to Flutter.

'It's not as if I'm handing you the keys to a brand new Roller, is it? Or, is there a reason I shouldn't trust your driving?'

'I don't think so. I admit I haven't driven for a while, but then, as you probably realise, there's not much call for it in prison, and I don't have a car of my own right now. But it's like riding a bike, isn't it? I'm sure I'll be fine once I get behind the wheel.'

Katie tossed the keys to him.

'We'll soon find out, won't we?'

'I'm not insured,' he said.

'This car's insured for any driver, so that's no excuse.'

'I'm not making excuses—'

'So, what are you waiting for? Get in and drive.'

Like a little boy on his best behaviour, Flutter carefully started the car, eased it into gear, and pulled away.

'There you go,' he said. 'Piece of cake. Where to, my lady?'

'A proper chauffeur would wear a uniform.'

'Yes, that's true enough,' said Flutter. 'But he'd also be given a decent car to drive.'

Katie laughed.

'Maybe in your dreams,' she said. 'But I'm afraid in real life you'll just have to get used to this one.'

Flutter followed Katie's directions in silent concentration and growing confidence, until she finally pointed to a turning on the left.

'Turn left here and drive down to the end of the road.'

Flutter did as directed and turned into what was a small trading estate. As they reached the end of the short road, she spoke again.

'My storage unit is the one on the right.'

Flutter slowed and pulled up. As he stopped the car, he squinted up at the building.

'It's a factory unit really,' she explained as they climbed from the car. 'They built this estate in the late 70s, but they overestimated the demand. It had been sitting empty for a couple of years when my dad made them a silly offer for the lease, and to his surprise they said yes.'

'I guess if you're stuck with an empty unit, any income is better than none,' said Flutter as they climbed from the car.

'The lease runs out soon,' she said as she slipped her key into the lock.

'What happens then?'

She shrugged.

'I move out.'

'Oh, right. Is there a lot of stuff?'

Katie pushed the door open and led the way inside, then stopped and made a sweeping gesture with her arm.

'Voila,' she said.

Flutter looked around. Floor to ceiling racks of old newspapers lined the longest wall. Racks of box files lined the remaining walls.

'Bloody hell,' he said.

'Quite,' she said with a wry smile.

'How far back does it go?'

'There are three copies of the newspaper from every week since 1926, minus a few editions during the war, so that's thousands of newspapers in total.'

Flutter ran his hand up over his forehead.

'Jesus!'

'I thought about asking for his help,' said Katie glumly, 'but I don't believe he's computer literate.'

'Sorry?'

'The only way I can keep it all is if I get it transferred into computer files, but that would take forever, and even then it wouldn't save the actual newspapers.'

'When does the lease run out?'

'Let's put it this way; if you had come to me in three months' time, there would have been no archive to search.'

Flutter studied Katie's face. He could see how upset she was at the thought of losing the archive, but he couldn't think of any words of comfort to offer.

'I don't know what to say,' he admitted.

'It's okay,' she said. 'I didn't expect you to have an answer. To be honest, I don't think there is one. I'll just have to get rid of it all.'

She let out a long sigh, then put on a brave smiley face and turned to him.

'Talking about something I can't change won't get us anywhere, will it? Where are these over-suits? I can't wait to try one on.'

Flutter handed her one of the blue paper suits.

'I see what you mean about looking ridiculous,' she said, five minutes later.

'Yes, but it's better than getting covered in crap,' said Flutter, now clad in a fetching blue over-suit of his own. 'As it's your archive, I'll let you be chief Smurf. So, where shall we start?'

'Why don't you look through the 1960 newspapers to see if there's any story that mentions Reggie or his funeral? I will see if I can find anything in classifieds.'

Flutter looked at the wall full of racks, wondering where he would find 1960.

'Can you give me a clue?'

She pointed to a corner.

'1926 is in that bottom left-hand corner. Everything goes from left to right, and then up one level.' She moved her arm to point again, but to the right and higher up. 'So it's probably somewhere up there.'

Flutter rubbed his hands together.

'Right, have you got a step-ladder?'

'Hang on, before you start.'

She reached into her bag, produced two face masks, and held one out to him.

He looked doubtful.

'You need to put it on,' she insisted. 'It's really dusty. Trust me, I know what I'm talking about.'

Reluctantly, he took the mask.

'Stepladder?' he asked.

'In that little room at the back,' she said. 'I've got a flask of tea in my bag. Let's do shifts of an hour, then take a fifteen minute break.'

Flutter nodded as he set off for the stepladder.

'That sounds like a plan.'

An hour later, Katie led Flutter back outside into fresh air and warm sunshine. They had brought two folding chairs from inside and now they sat sipping at the tea she had provided.

'Is it dusty enough for you?' she asked.

He smiled.

'Yeah, you were right about the mask.'

'It's awful, isn't it? That's one thing I won't miss when it's all gone.'

'Is there no way you can save it all?'

'But is it worth saving?' she asked. 'I come here about once a year and, as the owner of a sinking ship of a business, I have to put aside all sentimentality and face up to facts. Frankly, it's always been a luxury, and it has to go. Anyway, enough about that. Did you find anything?'

'I've done January through to April but not found any reference to Reggie yet. I reckon it will take all morning to go through the entire year. Have you had any luck?'

'Not yet,' she said, 'but its early days.'

They had been back inside on their second shift for half an hour when Katie tapped him on the shoulder. She had a sheet of paper in her hand.

'I've found the first "In Memoriam" notice. It was placed in October 1965.'

Flutter felt a wave of irritation. Was she telling him he'd been looking in the wrong place?

'I thought I was supposed to be looking at 1960?'

'Yes, that's right,' she said.

'But you just said 1965.'

He couldn't see her mouth because of the mask, but her eyes were smiling at his annoyance.

'Yes, I did, and that's because this was placed five years after they buried him.'

Now Flutter was grateful for the face mask hiding his red face.

'Ah, right, of course,' he said, sheepishly. 'October, you say? In that case, I'll skip the summer months for now and start in September. Do you know who placed the notice?'

'It's hand-written, but there's no name. It was on top when I opened the file. I'm hoping I can find more detail further down.'

'Oh well, it's a start,' said Flutter, moving the step ladder along the racks. 'Let's see if I can find a story to go with it.'

'Careful you don't choke on that slice of humble pie,' she said as she turned away.

He turned to reply, but the moment had gone and, anyway, she had been far too quick for him.

'It's nearly 3 o'clock,' said Katie. 'I think we should call it a day. Don't forget you have to get back.'

Flutter looked like a ghost, covered from head to foot in a grey dust. He even had cobwebs clinging to his back.

'I can't find a trace of him anywhere,' said Flutter.

'All I've got is a note saying they had booked the notice annually until this year, but there's no mention of a name to go with the booking. Apparently, whoever it was, paid in cash. My dad must have known who set it up.'

'All those years? Is that normal?'

'We have had some that are set up in advance, but for so long is unusual.'

'Maybe he did someone a deal, as a favour.'

'That's what I was thinking. I assume it must have been a woman, but who she is and why he owed her a favour, I don't know.'

Maybe he was being cynical, but there was one answer that came immediately into Flutter's head. If he was right, it could open a whole new can of worms that would probably persuade Katie to view her father in a less favourable light. He decided, unless it had some bearing on the case, he would keep his own counsel about reasons.

'I think you're right,' he said. 'Let's call it a day.'

As he began to remove his suit, he spoke again.

'Tomorrow, I'll check out the booking you found and see where that leads. I can always come back here if needs be.'

Katie stopped, half in and half out of the over-suit.

'What's with, "I" can do this, and "I" can do that?' she asked indignantly. 'I said I'd help, and I meant it. Besides, I found the booking, so I should be the one who gets to check it out.'

'Yeah, but you have a business to run.'

'I already told you my business is as good as finished,' she puffed, finally struggling free from the suit. 'Besides, I have something else planned for tomorrow.'

'I only said you can be chief Smurf while we're in the suits.'

Katie frowned and crossed her arms.

'Ah, yes, but whose the one with the office and the resources?'

Her smile proved her indignation was fake.

'Well, yeah, I'll give you that,' said Flutter. 'I don't have an office or a computer. And, let's be honest, you're the one with the brains around here.'

Flutter watched the pleasure on her face. He was a great believer that a little flattery could go a long way. Looking at her now, red-faced after struggling out of the suit, he realised she was the first woman he had felt comfortable with in a long time.

'All right then, boss,' he said, as they gathered their things together and made for the door. 'What's this plan for tomorrow?'

'I thought we could check out the cemetery. Let's see if we can find Reggie's grave.'

'It won't tell us what happened to him.'

'No,' she agreed, unlocking the car. 'But we don't even know if it's really out there. No offence, but we've only got the Duck Lady's word. I'm sure she's telling the truth, but you should always check what you've been told is fact, and not fiction, before you get carried away and waste a lot of time investigating. It's basic stuff, really.'

Flutter was about to jump in to defend Alma, but as he climbed into the car, he thought better of it.

'You're right,' he said. 'I probably would have been charging all over the place before it occurred to me to check anything. And it proves my point about which one of us should be the boss.'

'I learned the hard way that people who appear to be the most well-meaning are often the ones most willing to fill your head with bullshit if it suits their purpose,' said Katie as she started the car and pulled away.

Fifteen minutes later, they were back in the car park near Katie's office.

'I'd better get going or I'll be late. Usual time at the office in the morning?'

'I've got a few things to do first thing,' said Katie. 'Why don't we meet at the cemetery, say at 10:30ish?'

'I'll be there.'

Flutter climbed from the car, raised a hand in farewell, and set off across the car park towards the High Street. Katie watched him turn left onto the High Street and thought about following him to make sure he wasn't meeting his mystery woman again. But, as she climbed wearily from her car, she realised how wrong that would be, and how she would be furious if he spied on her. So, instead, she turned right when she got to the street and then right again through the doorway and up the stairs to her office.

Meanwhile, as Flutter sauntered down the High Street, his mobile phone rang. He fumbled it from his pocket and raised it to his ear.

'Hallo?'

'Harvey? It's Jenny Rodgers.'

'There's no need to be so formal, Jen.'

'Actually, there's every need to be formal and, as I told you before, you should address me as Mrs Rodgers.'

'I thought you said I should regard you as my friend. Friends don't call each other Mr and Mrs, do they?'

'I know it's short notice, but I'm afraid I'm going to have to postpone our meeting. The decorators are still here and the offices are such a mess they're unusable.'

'Oh, right, I get it,' said Flutter. 'So, I mustn't miss a meeting, on pain of death, but you can miss one at five minutes' notice whenever it suits you. Is that it?'

'Look, I'm sorry, but I haven't got time to argue with you now. Why don't I come to your house on Saturday morning, and we can have the meeting there?'

'You mean you want another informal meeting?'

'It'll kill two birds with one stone, and it means we won't fall any further behind,' she said.

'Of course not. Saturday morning will be fine. What time suits you?'

'Around ten-thirty?'

'I'll be there,' said Flutter. 'There's a buzzer by the gate. Press it and I'll open the gates so you can drive up to the house.'

CHAPTER 8

Friday

At ten thirty on the dot, Flutter walked through the gates of the cemetery. Katie was just two minutes behind him. Although she was desperate to know if Flutter had been with his mystery girlfriend again, she was determined not to show it and would avoid the subject unless he raised it. Of course, if that happened, it would be absolutely fine to use all her interviewing skills to extract every scrap of information she could.

In the meantime, she would play it cool and try to behave normally. To get started, they needed to decide how they would approach the search.

'Shouldn't there be a plan somewhere, or a book that lists the location of every grave?' suggested Flutter.

'I called the vicar this morning,' said Katie. 'I couldn't decide if he was the most unhelpful person I have ever encountered, or the most disorganised. Anyway, according to him, the only thing they have is a tatty old map that shows the layout, and a book that lists graves but only after 1999. If you want to find anything before that, you're on your own.'

'But I thought this cemetery has been here for donkey's years.'

'So it has but, apparently, there was a fire in 1998 which destroyed all the old records. He said he'd like to come and help us, but he has a wedding to prepare for. To be honest, I thought we'd probably manage better on our own, anyway.'

'D'you think it's worth talking to him again?'

'He only came here in 2009, so I don't think he can offer us anything new.'

'You're probably right,' agreed Flutter, 'but we'll keep him in mind, just in case.'

He rubbed his hands together enthusiastically, then looked across the cemetery. It seemed to stretch away forever, and his shoulders slumped as his enthusiasm drained away.

'Don't start getting gloomy before we've even started,' said Katie. 'You're supposed to be the Happy Chappy with a joke for every occasion, aren't you?'

'I'm not getting gloomy. I was just thinking the sooner we find this grave, the sooner you can buy me lunch.'

He offered her his best cheeky grin, but she remained unmoved.

'I don't think I've got time for that today.'

'Oh, right. Okay, no problem.'

She reached in her handbag, pulled out two small nailbrushes, and handed one to him.

'You might need one of these. They're a bit on the small side, but it was the best I could do.'

'What's this for?' he asked. 'Are you worried I'll get my nails dirty?'

'Most of these headstones are covered in dirt, and moss, and stuff,' said Katie, abruptly. 'You can use the brush to clean them off. It'll make them easier to read.'

Flutter thought this made perfect sense and wondered why such practical ideas never occurred to him. He also wondered why Katie was in such a crabby mood, but after the way she had jumped down his throat on Monday afternoon, he thought better of asking her. If she didn't want to share, he wasn't going to pry.

They chose to start by the gates and follow the path that ran through the middle of the cemetery, and then take the outer path that went all the way around the perimeter, searching through the graves on each side as they went.

They walked on in silence for a while, studying the headstones. Flutter was pleased to find the cemetery wasn't as extensive as he had first thought. It had only taken twenty minutes to walk the length of the path, and he estimated it would only take an hour and a half, at most, to finish the search.

'Which way?' he asked when they reached the end of the centre path.

'Right,' suggested Katie.

They turned right and began walking.

'You're quiet,' she said.

'Yeah, well, when the atmosphere's explosive I find it's usually best not to light a match.'

Katie bristled.

'What's that supposed to mean?'

'I don't remember the weather forecast saying it was going to be so frosty.'

'Frosty?'

'You're not exactly a bundle of joy this morning, are you?'

She stared at him, but said nothing.

'We all wake up in a crappy mood from time to time,' said Flutter. 'I get that. I just don't think you should take it out on me, unless it's my fault. And if it is my fault, you should tell me what I've done.'

'I'm sorry. I suppose I have been touchy, but I thought you would be cracking jokes all the way round.'

'I think you'll find that was your idea,' said Flutter. 'I'm afraid I don't find much to laugh about in a graveyard.'

'There must be some way you can cheer me up.'

'And how am I supposed to do that?'

'You could tell me what's it's like being Flutter.'

'You already know what it's like. I get crapped on from a great height and end up in trouble that's often not of my own making.'

'Okay, so what were you doing before you went to prison?'

Flutter chuckled.

'Before? I'm not sure you want to know too much about that.'

Katie smiled.

'It can't have been that bad.'

'I did a lot of things I'm not proud of, like stealing and stuff.'

'Ah. I see what you mean. So what changed?'

'I got bored, things happened, I went to prison and realised I needed to change. And, right now, I'm feeling as if I'm being interviewed for a story.'

'Sorry. Am I being too nosey? It's just that I like to know what makes people tick.'

'I seem to recall telling you once before that I tick much better when I'm not having to answer loads of questions.'

She pulled a face and pouted.

'That's told me,' she said sulkily. 'All right Mr Grumpy, I'll try to keep quiet.'

'There's no need to sulk,' he said, relieved that her mood seemed to have improved. 'And you don't have to keep quiet; just don't ask so many questions.'

'Can I ask how old you are?'

Flutter sighed. He couldn't decide if she was amusing or annoying.

'Thirty-one if you really want to know, although I can't see what difference it makes.'

'Goodness, that makes you five years older than me!'

'Does it matter?' asked Flutter.

'Well, no, I suppose not. I was just curious.'

They had reached a corner where a dense cypress tree stood alongside the path.

'You don't believe in ghosts, do you?' she asked, stepping from the path to explore the nearby graves.

'Good God, no,' he said, 'but you can never be sure, can you?'

It was a deliberate tease to see what she would say, but she was crouching down, brushing at something, and didn't seem to have heard him. Then she stood up, her face excited.

'I think I've found him!'

Flutter hurried over to her.

'Here, this one,' she said, pointing down by her feet at a tiny headstone.

'Alma said there was no headstone, just a small cross,' he said doubtfully.

Katie hadn't cleared all the moss away, but now she scrubbed harder.

'Maybe the person who set up the memorial notice arranged for a headstone, too.'

A few seconds later, she stepped back.

'There you are, look,' she said. 'This must be the right one.'

Flutter felt a little shiver up his back. He couldn't see the full name, but he knew instinctively this was the right grave. Just as Alma had told him, it was at the back, in a corner, more or less hidden away where no-one would notice it. He crouched down and read the legend on the headstone.

REGINALD FULSHAW.
1940-1960

'If this guy died in active service in Malaysia,' said Flutter. 'Why is his grave tucked away out of sight like this?'

'Died a hero, buried a pauper,' said Katie. 'Something doesn't add up, does it?'

'So, what do we do now?' asked Flutter.

'If he died in active service, and was then buried quietly like this, there's got to be something fishy going on.'

'You mean like if friendly fire had killed him?'

'That could be one reason for a cover-up. And if he had no family, it would have been relatively easy to bring him back and quietly bury him, and bury his secret along with him.'

'But there must be records,' said Flutter.

'What, way back in the sixties? I told you before, even if there is a record, the Army isn't good at sharing its secrets. If this was an official police enquiry, you'd probably get nowhere, so what chance do you think we have as Joe Public? We're not even related.'

'I can at least ask.'

'If you get any response, it will probably be to tell you the records got lost when the Regiments were amalgamated. Seriously, you've got no chance.'

Flutter frowned.

'I thought if I can find out where his old mates are we could speak to them.'

'Don't look so disappointed. It's not the end of the road. I told you the Royal Hamshire was my uncle's old regiment.'

'D'you think he could help?'

'He's getting on now, and he doesn't always know what day it is, but his distant memories are clear enough. If I can catch him at the right time, you never know what he might remember.'

'How soon can you see him?'

'If you let me take the cap badge and photo, I could visit him over the weekend. If I show him the badge, it might trigger his memory.'

Flutter couldn't hide his surprise.

'Are you sure? I didn't expect you to drop everything for this.'

She smiled.

'Are you kidding? This could be the best thing I've done in months.

CHAPTER 9

SATURDAY

The enormous house in Willow Grove seemed even more daunting on Saturday morning but, by the time Jenny was due to arrive, Flutter had made sure the house looked presentable and was now sipping a cup of tea in the kitchen.

Winston was nearby, in his bed, doing an impression of the living dead. While they were living in the big house, the old dog had made a habit of rolling in anything remotely unpleasant he found in the garden. Since moving to the small house with its tiny garden, this habit had been curtailed and he had mostly smelt relatively inoffensive.

Unfortunately, this morning, without thinking, Flutter had made the mistake of letting him loose in the garden. Almost immediately, his nose had detected something particularly disgusting in a corner of the garden. It seems a fox who used the garden as a shortcut had left his calling card. Not content with just discovering the stinking mess, Winston had given in to his hound dog heritage and felt obliged to roll in it.

He had returned to the back door twenty minutes ago looking immensely pleased with himself, and it was only when Flutter got wind of the awful aroma that had accompanied the dog's return that he noticed the streaks of foul smelling fox excrement smeared across his back. It was as if Winston knew there was an important visitor due, and now, of course, it was too late to do anything about it.

Flutter had considered punishing the old dog by returning him to the garden and making him stay out there, but one look from those big sad eyes had made it impossible to enforce the penalty. Not for the first time in their brief relationship, Flutter had cursed his luck to have a dog that could manipulate his feelings so easily. In an attempt to subdue the aroma, Winston had been banished to his bed and covered with a blanket. A barrage of wheezy snores was a continual reminder of his presence.

It was now nearly 10:45. Jenny was late, and Flutter was becoming increasingly nervous. He could remember feeling like this the very first time he had arranged a date with her and had been waiting for her to arrive. She had been late that day, too, but he could still remember that feeling of despair when he thought she would not show, and then how his heart had nearly burst with joy when she had finally arrived.

The sound of the buzzer interrupted his recollections, warning him someone was at the gate. On the small screen in the hall, he could see Jenny's face at her car window.

'Hello,' he said into the speaker.

'Oh, so it is you,' said Jenny's surprised voice through the loudspeaker. 'I thought this would be another one of your terrible practical jokes.'

Flutter resisted the temptation to say "I told you so" and pressed the button to open the gates. He watched through the window until her car appeared, pressed the button to close the gates, and then opened the front door and stepped outside. Her face was a picture as she sat in the car and took in her surroundings, before eventually opening the car door and walking across to join him.

'It must be difficult for you to believe crime doesn't pay when you come home to this,' she said.

'Good morning, Mrs Rodgers,' said Flutter. 'It's very nice to see you, too.'

She looked at him as if he'd insulted her.

'I beg your pardon?'

'I thought it was your job to help me get my life back on track, not keep putting me down. As you know very well, I didn't get this house through the proceeds of crime. It was left to me, in a will, by my biological father. I can supply you with the solicitor's number so you can check my story, if you really want to.'

For a moment she didn't look so sure of herself, and seemed on the verge of tears, but then she managed a smile.

'I'm sorry. You're right. I'm afraid I've had a poor start to the day.'

'Are you all right?' he asked.

'Yes, I'm fine.'

He could see she wasn't at all fine, but kept his concern to himself.

He nodded at the driveway.

'How am I doing so far? Does my accommodation tick enough boxes for you?'

'It's very nice,' she said. 'Can I have a look inside?'

He stepped back to give her room.

'Go on in. Have a wander around while I make us a cup of tea.'

She didn't look too sure.

'You can go wherever you like,' he assured her. 'I've got nothing to hide.'

Cautiously, Jenny made her way into the house, pushing doors open and peering into each of the rooms, finishing up in the kitchen where Flutter was waiting at the table. There was room to sit next to him, but she deliberately put the table between them and sat opposite him.

'I wish someone would leave me a house like this,' she said wistfully.

'You've changed your mind about it being a game, then? It even came with a housekeeper.'

'Seriously? You have a housekeeper?'

'She came with the house. It was a condition of the will. She had an apartment above the garage, but she moved out to look after her aunt.'

'It looks as though your father thought of everything.'

'Yeah, everything except being an actual father.'

Flutter pointed to the dog bed, where Winston snored contentedly beneath his blanket.

'I've even inherited his dog.'

'Why is he covered with a blanket?'

'He stinks. He must have rolled in something out in the garden. I think it was a present from the local fox. I didn't have time to stick him in the shower, so the blanket's there to stifle the smell.'

'I wondered what the awful smell was, but I didn't like to ask.'

'If you think it's bad now, let's hope he doesn't wake up and come over here. He must have known you were coming.'

She gave him a disapproving look.

'What's that supposed to mean?'

'Nothing. I just meant it was typical of my luck that he should choose this morning to get all stinky. It's as if he wanted to make sure I didn't make a good impression.'

'Don't worry. You're doing fine so far.'

She had been carrying her briefcase when she had arrived, and now she opened it and removed his file, placed it on the table and flipped it open.

'Let's get started,' she said. 'Now, first, I want to talk about this job of yours.'

'What about it?'

'Well, how did you get it?'

'Didn't she tell you when you spoke to her?'

'Yes, but I want to hear it from you.'

Flutter rolled his eyes.

'Okay. So, I bumped into this woman who owns the newspaper. We got talking, and it turned out she needed someone to do some odd jobs now and then. I'm quite good at handyman stuff, and I was interested, so she offered me the job.'

'It seems a bit of a casual arrangement, doesn't it?'

'But I've got an allowance through the will. It's not as if I'm struggling to survive, is it?'

'You don't think this woman's taking advantage of your situation?'

'What situation?'

'Just out of prison, looking for a job. I'm just worried you might be used as cheap labour.'

Flutter smiled.

'What d'you mean you're worried about me?'

'I'm speaking from a professional point of view,' she said hastily. 'Anyway, that's not the point. You're supposed to be telling me who this woman is, and why she offered you a job.'

'I just told you. She runs the local newspaper.'

'All right. Let's start with, how did you really meet her?'

'I'm sorry?'

'Last time we met, you told me you went to her office. She says you met over a cup of coffee.'

Just for a moment, Flutter froze, but he didn't think Katie had shopped him; Jenny was far too calm for that.

'Oh, well, yeah, we first met in the coffee shop. She knew I was a stranger in town, so she started talking to me.'

'Why would she do that?'

'I don't know. Maybe it's because I'm so amazingly charismatic, or because she enjoys meeting people, or perhaps she's just plain nosey. I already told you she's a journalist; I suppose it goes with the job.'

'And she offered you a job on the strength of a chance meeting in a coffee shop?'

'She didn't offer me a job until later.'

'How much later?'

'I went to her office and asked if she could help me find out who my dad was.'

'Why would you ask someone you hardly know to do that?'

'I asked her because she's a journalist. She runs the local newspaper, and it's her job to find things out.'

'But why would she do that for you?'

'Why not?'

'How do you know she won't use what she finds in a story?'

'I don't, but she told me she wouldn't, and I trust her.'

'Did you pay her?'

'No. She just looked through the records to see if they had anything that might shed some light on who he was.'

'And did it?'

'Yeah, a bit.'

'Are you sure you can trust her?'

'After being locked away for a year for something I didn't do, I'm not sure I can trust anyone so, what have I got to lose?'

'Okay, but this job she's offering you isn't exactly a career, is it?'

'Jen, I've just come out of prison. How many people are going to offer me a career?'

'I could put you on to some people.'

'Yeah, I'm sure you could, but they're exactly the people who will exploit me. Look, I don't need the money, and the house is paid for.'

'Which house?'

'Both of them.'

She stared hard at him, trying to work out if he was trying to be clever, but Flutter wasn't backing down.

'Do you like her?'

'Yeah, I do. She's a "what you see is what you get" sort of person. I feel I know where I stand with her, and I like that.'

She studied his face again, but ignored the implied slight.

'Do you find her attractive?'

'What sort of question is that?'

'Well, do you?'

'Would that be a problem?'

'No, I suppose not,' she said, hastily.

'Anyway, if you're worried about that, it's not an issue; she has a boyfriend.'

'I told you; I'm just concerned she's not trying to take advantage of you.'

'It sounds like you're more concerned I might try to take advantage of her.'

'Don't be silly.'

'If you must know, I like her a lot, but not because I want to get inside her knickers,' he said pointedly. 'It's because, since I got out of prison, she's the only person I've met who hasn't put me down and seems to be prepared to give me a chance. To me, that counts for a lot.'

She licked her lips, and Flutter braced himself for another lecture, but to his surprise, it didn't happen.

'I'm sorry if I've given you that impression,' she said. 'I didn't mean to. Perhaps I've not been as fair as I should be. Maybe you'd be better off with someone else as your supervisor.'

'What? No way. I don't want someone else. I want you!'

As soon as the words had left his mouth, Flutter realised what he was implying. He hadn't meant for it to come out quite like that, but, looking at her face, he couldn't tell how she'd taken it. For a moment he thought about apologising, but he'd said it now, and he couldn't take it back, could he? And anyway, it was the truth. It would be hypocritical to apologise.

Embarrassed, Jenny looked down at her notes. Flutter braced himself for another lecture about keeping their relationship strictly professional, but to this surprise, it didn't happen. For almost a minute she didn't speak, but the silence was too much for Flutter to bear.

'Can I ask you a personal question?'

'That depends what it is,' she said without looking up.

'Your husband. Do I know him?'

'You might. His name's Jed Rodgers. I believe he would have been two or three years above you at school.'

'Really? You married Jed Rodgers? I seem to recall he was the school bully, wasn't he?'

'I wouldn't know about that. I didn't go to that school.'

'You would have known him if you went to our school. Everyone knew Jed, and nearly everyone feared him.'

There was a brief, awkward silence, then Jenny sat back and placed her hands on the table. She wore several large bangles on her left wrist, but if they were supposed to hide the bruising, they failed miserably. A few seconds passed before she noticed Flutter was staring at the wrist. Hastily, she pulled her sleeve down to cover it.

'That's a nasty bruise,' he said.

Defiantly, she looked him in the eye.

'It's nothing,' she said. 'I tripped and put my hands out to save myself. Better a bruised wrist than smacking my head on the floor.'

'Yeah, some bruises are much easier to hide than others,' said Flutter. 'Any bully would know that.'

'I'm sorry?'

'Jed was a bully when he was at school, and it looks as if he still is.'

'I don't know what you're talking about.'

'Yes you do,' said Flutter.

'It's none of your business, and I'd like it to stay that way.'

'If he's knocking you about—'

'I think I'd better go now,' she said.

Before he had realised what he was doing, Flutter had reached across the table and taken her hand. Now they both stared down at the hand and then up at each other, but Flutter could see she was furious. He snatched his hand away as if hers had been red hot.

'Shit! I'm sorry,' he said. 'I don't know why I did that.'

She was staring at him, still looking angry, but she said nothing. Flutter thought this was a sure sign she was about to tear into him.

'Jenny. I'm really, really sorry. I shouldn't have done that. I don't know what came over me. Well, I do. It's the thought of that thug knocking you around. But I understand if I upset you, and I'm sorry.'

'I'd better go.'

'Please don't let this change things,' he said, desperately. 'I don't want anyone else as my supervisor. Can't we just forget this happened? It won't happen again, trust me.'

'I trusted you once before,' she said sternly. 'Remember?'

He hung his head.

'Remember? Jesus, if only I could forget! My life is littered with dumb mistakes, but that's the one I regret more than any other. If I could turn the clock back...'

'Yes, well, I'm afraid none of us can do that, can we? And if we could, I can assure you I'd be up there at the head of the queue. As my mother once told me, I chose my bed, and now I have to lie in it.'

'Eh?'

'She thinks I've made a mess of my life.'

'That's funny. She told me I'd done that once,' said Flutter. 'Does she mean Jed?'

She looked as if she was about to tell him, but then she seemed to change her mind.

'I'd better go. He'll be wondering where I've got to.'

She stood up.

Flutter stood up and stepped in front of her, but to his horror, she flinched and tried to back away. There was barely a foot between them, and now he reached for her. Hesitantly, she looked up at him, then stepped forward into his arms and sobbed quietly.

'Jesus, you're terrified of him, aren't you?' he said, stroking her hair. 'You can't live like this. It's not right.'

'And what else can I do?' she asked.

'You could leave him and come and live with me.'

'And have him camped outside waiting for me? It would be like exchanging one prison for another. It wouldn't work. If it was that simple, I would have left a long time ago.'

'But we have to do something?'

Now she took a step back.

'There is no "we",' she said. 'This is my problem, and I'm handling it my way.'

'If you don't mind me saying, your way hasn't worked so far, has it?'

'I won't have you involved. I know you want to help, but it wouldn't end well for either of us.'

'I'm not frightened of Jed. I never was.'

'Oh, wonderful. Stupid bravado. That's all I need. What are you going to do, arrange a duel?'

'I'll fight him if that's what it takes.'

'D'you really want to go back to prison? If you start a war with him, that's where you'll end up. Either that or he'd kill us both before it came to that. In fact, he'll probably kill us both if he finds out I've been to see you today.'

'He doesn't know you're here?'

'He doesn't even know you're my client, and he mustn't find out.'

'Why not?'

'He hates you.'

'Why? What did I ever do to him?'

'You had me before him.'

She left Flutter to think about that as she gathered her things and headed for the front door.

'Thank you for showing me around your house. It's beautiful.'

Flutter opened the door for her and followed her out to her car.

'We need to book another meeting,' she said. My office is still not ready, so can we meet in Leslie's again?'

'Sure. When?'

'How about Friday morning, around 11:00?'

'I'll be there,' said Flutter, as she climbed into her car.

'I want to help you, Jenny,' he said. 'If you won't leave him, at least let me be someone you can turn to for help. I owe you that much.'

'We'll see,' she said.

'Here, take this,' he said, pulling a piece of paper from his pocket and handing it to her.

'What is it?'

'It's the entry codes for this place. I keep a copy in case I forget them.'

'Don't you need it?'

'I've got another copy at home. Anyway, think about what I said. If you need to leave him, you could always hide out here for a few days.'

'I'm not going to leave him.'

'But you might change your mind.'

She closed the car door, started the engine, and slowly drove down to the gates. Flutter watched as she waited for the gates to open, hoping she might look back so they could exchange a parting smile or wave goodbye, but she drove off without a second glance.

CHAPTER 10

SUNDAY

After spending a couple of hours with her great-uncle on Sunday afternoon, Katie headed for home. When she got back, she called on/off boyfriend Detective Sergeant Robbie Bright and offered to cook dinner for him if he came round later that evening. Bright couldn't believe his luck and, just as Katie had hoped, he jumped at the chance.

By 9pm they had eaten and were cosily settled on her sofa, each with a glass of wine in hand. Bright was convinced there could only be one way for the night to end, but Katie had other intentions, and it wasn't long before she steered the conversation in the direction she wanted.

'A friend of mine told me about this guy who died doing his National Service. He was an orphan, with no family. He's buried in the cemetery here in Waterbury. The thing is, every year someone places one of those In Memoriam notices in the local paper on the anniversary of his death.'

'As far as I'm aware, there's no law against remembering someone whose no longer with us.'

'Yeah, that bit's okay, but here's where it gets weird: someone placed a notice announcing his funeral. It's next Monday.'

Bright rolled his eyes.

'And your point is?'

'The man died in Malaysia in 1960 and was buried here the same year. There's a grave bearing his name in the cemetery!'

'He died in Malaysia? In 1960? I'm sorry, but I don't see why this should concern either of us. Didn't you say he was in the Army? Don't you think the Military Police would have investigated his death if there was anything suspicious about it?'

'My great-uncle says there's a possibility local bandits killed him.'

'How would your great-uncle know?'

'He was in the same regiment.'

'Well, there you are, then. Case closed.'

'Don't you think it's funny he's being buried again?'

'There's probably been a mistake. Do you know how many misprints and cock-ups are published in local papers every week?'

'Not in my local newspaper,' said Katie indignantly.

'I didn't mean it's your fault,' said Bright, hastily. 'It sounds as if the person who placed the notice got it wrong.'

'Yes, but what if it isn't a cock-up? My friend says—'

'This friend of yours wouldn't be your detective partner, Flipper, would it?'

'His name is Flutter.'

'Whatever. I'm not here to investigate things just because he says so. If you two are serious about playing amateur detectives, why don't you investigate it yourselves?'

'We're going to. I just thought you might help.'

'I'm a professional detective, Katie, doing a proper job. I haven't got time to mess about for you, and especially not for him!'

Katie pouted.

'I know you don't like him, but I thought, as you like me, and you moved here to be nearer to me—'

'Oh, hang on,' said Bright, an evil glint in his eyes. 'Now I see what's going on here. When you invited me to dinner, you said you were missing me, but the truth is you only invited me here so you can try to twist me round your little finger.'

'That's not true.'

'Oh, come on, Katie, you know very well that's exactly what it is. You want me to drop everything so I can run unauthorised searches, and who knows what else, to investigate something that might have happened yonks ago, halfway around the world. And all because your friend Flipper says so. If you really believe I'm gullible enough to fall for this, you must think I'm as thick as shit.'

He got to his feet and stomped off to find his coat and shoes. Katie had known there was a good chance Bright would see through her, but she would not give up just yet. She followed him out to the hall where he was putting his shoes on.

'Don't go,' she said, but he ignored her and continued tying his shoelaces.

'I don't expect you to drop everything, but you have to admit it's weird,' she said.

Bright's face was turning red as he got to his feet and reached for his coat.

'What's weird, Katie, is that you think it would be a simple matter to find out what happened in Malaysia over sixty years ago, and that you think I can just drop everything because you and Flipper say so.'

'But if anyone can do it, you can. You're a brilliant detective.'

'You don't need a detective for something like that, Katie, you need Doctor bloody Who!'

'So, you're not interested in helping, then?'

'Oh. You've finally got it, have you?' said Bright, with as much sarcasm as he could muster.

'And you're not interested in staying over?'

'Staying over? You mean...'

'I know things haven't gone quite the way you were hoping, and I know that's probably my fault, so I thought we could make a new start.'

'Really?'

'Really.'

Bright studied her face for a moment before he replied.

'Sorry, Katie, but as tempting as your offer is, it won't work,' said Bright.

'But I thought you wanted to…'

'Oh, believe me, I do, more than anything, but you're not taking me for a fool any longer.'

'But I'm not taking you for a fool, Robbie.'

'Oh, but you are,' he said, reaching for the door handle. 'I left all my old mates behind when I moved down here to be with you. I don't see any of them now, and I've barely set eyes on you, either. And when I do see you, all you talk about is your jailbird friend, Flipper!'

'It's Flutter.'

'There, you see. You even think it's important I get his stupid name right!'

'Please, let's not do this again. I understand you're annoyed with me and you don't want to stay over tonight, but you'll feel differently tomorrow. Why not come and stay for a couple of nights in the week, and let's start again?'

Bright opened the door and stepped outside.

'I couldn't, even if I wanted to,' he said. 'I'm on a training course all week.'

'Well, call me when you get back. Please.'

'I'll think about it,' he said, then turned and walked away.

Katie stepped inside, closed the door and leaned back against it. She had been in an on/off relationship with Robbie Bright for the best part of three years, and yet she wasn't particularly upset at the idea that it might the over for good. Perhaps that told her all she needed to know.

CHAPTER 11

MONDAY

It had been a few weeks since he had been released from prison, but Flutter was still coming to terms with being free and was keen to take advantage of any excuse to exercise that freedom. This morning he walked to the park and handed Winston on to Doris a little earlier than normal, intending to familiarise himself with more of Waterbury.

Instead of heading straight for the High Street, he had walked some of the back streets. It did not surprise him to find much of the area behind the town centre had been redeveloped, as in so many towns. Where rows of tiny terraced houses had once stood, there was now a long, narrow car park. It was bordered on one side by a six-storey block of flats, and the other by a similarly tall office block.

As he took in the surroundings, Flutter realised this was the car park that serviced the shops on the High Street, and the offices above them, including Katie's. This meant he should be able to access the High Street through the other side of the car park.

Without thinking, he stepped off the kerb, only to hear the loud beeping of a car horn, causing him to take swift evasive action to avoid being run down. As the car swept past him, the angry driver seemed to be almost snarling as he aimed a finger at Flutter and cursed his stupidity. But Flutter didn't really notice the driver. It was the frightened face staring at him from the passenger seat that caught his attention.

Making sure the road was clear this time, Flutter crossed the car park, watching the car as it sped around the perimeter of the car park, and pulled up on the other side. It was barely fifty yards from one side of the car park to the other, and Flutter was already halfway across. He could see the driver was berating the passenger, who seemed to be almost shrinking into her seat under the verbal onslaught.

Finally, they climbed from the car, and the man, Jed Rodgers, stomped around to the back of the vehicle. He raised the boot and waited for the woman to reach inside and collect her bags.

'All right, Jenny?' called Flutter, as he reached them.

The man swung around and glared at him.

'Who the hell are you?'

'I'm just saying hello,' said Flutter. 'Is that a problem?'

'I dunno. You tell me. Is it?'

Jed looked at Jenny, who looked as though she would like the ground to open up and swallow her, then he looked back at Flutter and, at that moment, everything suddenly clicked into place for him.

'Wait a minute,' said Jed, a thin smile creasing his face. 'You're Flutter Gamble, aren't you?'

'What can I say?' said Flutter, disarmingly. 'Guilty as charged.'

Now Jed turned on Jenny, who flinched as he shouted at her.

'This is why you sneaked out of the house on Saturday morning without telling me where you were going, is it?'

'I told you, I was working,' she said.

'A likely story,' said Jed. 'I ought to bloody—'

'Here, hang on a minute, mate,' said Flutter. 'That's no way to speak to a lady.'

'Lady?' roared Jed. 'She's no lady, she's just a cheap—'

Jed made a lunge for Jenny, but Flutter stepped in between them.

'Harvey, leave it,' said Jenny. 'It doesn't matter.'

'Oh, it matters,' said Flutter. 'It matters a lot!'

'Please don't,' pleaded Jenny. 'Just leave it. You'll only make things worse.'

'She's my wife,' snarled Jed. 'I can talk to her how I like.'

'That's not quite how it works, mate,' said Flutter, bravado now controlling his thinking. 'I think someone needs to teach you some manners.'

Jed was taller, heavier, and appeared much stronger than Flutter, and now he laughed in his face.

'Oh, yeah? Come on then, Mr Hard Man. I'd like to see you try!'

Jenny tugged at Jed's arm.

'Stop it, both of you!'

Jed swatted her away, and she barely kept her feet as she stumbled from the blow.

'Right. That's it,' said Flutter. 'I've had enough. I will not stand here and let you treat her like that.'

Jed's eyes lit up at the prospect of a fight, and a cruel smile creased his face.

'Oh yeah? Come on, then. Let's see what you've got.'

Flutter swallowed hard and took a step back. He wasn't a fighter, and he hadn't expected Jed to rise to the challenge so eagerly. Inwardly, he cursed his big mouth as he took another step back to put a bit more space between himself and Jed, who seemed to have suddenly become even bigger.

As fights go, it didn't last long. Flutter had thought Jed would be slow, as he was so big, but in this, he was sadly mistaken. Before he even saw it coming, a massive right fist landed in his face. The punch sent him flying, and he suddenly found himself in a heap on the ground, his head buzzing and his left eye throbbing.

Flutter braced himself for a kicking as Jed took a step towards him, but instead, Jed uttered a warning.

'I'd really love to stay and batter the crap out of you right now, Flutter, but I'm busy this morning,' he said. 'But don't think this is over. When I get a spare five minutes, I'll be coming to kick your head in, and you won't see me coming.'

With that, he jumped back into his car and drove away.

Jenny watched him drive off, then rushed over to Flutter and knelt down by him.

'Are you okay?' she asked.

Flutter put a hand to his face and gingerly felt for bumps and bruises.

'I've had better starts to the day, but I'll survive,' he said.

'Does it hurt?' asked Jenny. 'I'm surprised he only punched you the one time.'

'Yeah, I was a bit surprised myself,' said Flutter ruefully. 'I didn't think he could move that fast.'

'You're lucky. At least you saw it coming. Normally, he attacks people when they're not looking.'

Flutter took his hand away from his face.

'I didn't see that punch coming, and I certainly don't feel lucky. Bruised is a better word for how I feel right now. Both my face and my ego.'

'Here, give me your hand,' she said.

He reached out, and she helped him to his feet.

'Let me help you get cleaned up,' she said.

'I'm fine,' he said.

'No, you're not,' she said. 'At least let me see if we have something for that eye.'

'You shouldn't have to put up with that sort of behaviour from him, Jen. It's just not right. You should leave him.'

'Yes, well, thank you for your advice, but I'm afraid it's not that simple.'

'Yes, it is. You just pack your bags and walk out.'

'And where would I go?'

'You could come and live with me. I've got plenty of room.'

'Don't you think that would be the first place he would come looking? You can't help me. No-one can.'

'That's not true, I can hel—'

'I don't want you to get involved. You could end up back in prison, and I don't want that to happen.'

'Jed wants to be careful. Sooner or later, someone's going to give him a dose of his own medicine and attack him when he's not looking.'

'If that's a threat, I hope you don't intend to carry it out.'

'Someone has to stop him.'

'Well, it had better not be you. I know Jed. He won't just punch you once and walk off next time. It'll be much worse. He might even kill you!'

'Come on, Jen. Kill me? Really?'

'Don't joke about it, Harvey. I wouldn't put it past him.'

CHAPTER 12

Half an hour later, Flutter and Katie were perched on stools looking out at the world from inside the coffee shop. Flutter's eye was half-closed and rapidly turning various shades of black and blue and, so far, he could not convince Katie how it had happened.

'And you really expect me to believe you walked into a door?' she asked.

'I told you, I was rushing. I nipped through the door and forgot it swings shut, and on the way back, I ran straight into it.'

'And this was a round door, was it?'

'Sorry?'

'All the doors in my house have straight edges. If I banged my head on one, I would expect to have a long, straight bruise. I'm no expert, but I would say your bruise is more sort of fist-shaped.'

'You know I can't afford to risk getting into a fight. Any sort of trouble like that and I could end up back in prison. Anyway, I'm not a bloke who starts fights.'

'I didn't say you started it and, anyway, it's only a fight if you hit back. Otherwise, it's an assault. If someone has assaulted you, report them to the police.'

'Okay,' said Flutter. 'I tell you what. If it makes you happy, you can report my kitchen door for assaulting me. But I think you'll find the police might not take too kindly to you wasting their time like that.'

She studied his face. She knew he was hiding something, but he wasn't budging from his story.

'Okay,' she said. 'You stick to your stupid story that you walked into a door if you must, but don't think I'm fooled by it. We both know it's not true, and I will find out what really happened.'

'There's nothing to find out.'

'Perhaps I'll ask Robbie if anyone has reported seeing an assault take place.'

'That's not a good idea, is it?'

'Why not?'

'Why d'you think? If you tell him I've been in anything like a fight, he could use it as an excuse to cause me lots of grief. Is that what you want?'

'Well, no, of course not.'

'Well then, let it go. I'm just a little bruised, that's all. It'll all be gone in a couple of days, and we'll have forgotten all about it.'

Katie knew she was wasting her time arguing with him, so she changed the subject.

'I went to see my great-uncle yesterday.'

'How was he?' asked Flutter.

'The poor old fellow isn't doing very well, but he was fairly lucid once I showed him the cap badge.'

'Did he know anything?'

'He says he wasn't posted out there until 1961. Apparently, the Army moved out of Malaysia in 1963 and he was sent there to make sure it was a smooth withdrawal. He says he's not aware of any scandal in his time out there, but can't vouch for what might have happened before. He did recall security being tight because bandits had killed a young soldier the year before he arrived, but again, he didn't know any details.'

'Not much help then?'

'I got the impression he knows more, but he was cagey and wouldn't say what it was. I'm sorry, but I can only push him so hard.'

'There's no need to apologise. I understand the situation.'

'I'm also up against his loyalty to the Regiment. I think that would stop him telling me anything, even if he wasn't ill.'

'Oh, well, it was worth a try.'

'It wasn't a complete disaster. He had two regimental photographs, and being the type he is, he even had a list of all the names. So, I think I've found the surnames of the other two half backs in the football team.'

'Oh, wow, that's fantastic,' said Flutter.

'Don't get too excited. We still don't know where they live, or even if they're still alive.'

'There's probably a good chance they're no longer alive,' said Flutter gloomily. 'They must have been around the same age as Reggie, which means they must be in their eighties.'

'I told Robbie about Reggie last night,' said Katie. 'I thought he might help.'

'Oh yeah. What did he say?'

'Basically, he thinks we're wasting our time. He said the police had better things to do than investigate a funeral notice that is probably a simple mistake, and they certainly wouldn't entertain the idea of re-investigating something that happened over sixty years ago in a country where they have no jurisdiction.'

'And of course, he wouldn't help me, even if it was a matter of life and death,' said Flutter with a wry smile.

'I was annoyed with him at the time, but I suppose he's got a point,' said Katie. 'However weird announcing a funeral for someone whose already buried might seem I can't think there's a law against it. And for all we know, it might be a genuine mistake. As for what might have happened in Malaysia back in 1960, well, whose to say bandits didn't kill him?'

Flutter sighed.

'Yeah, I suppose you're right,' he said. 'But I promised Alma I'd look into it, and I don't feel I can stop now. I can't let a dying woman down.'

'I'm not suggesting we should stop,' said Katie. 'In fact, I started searching for our two footballers last night.'

'Any luck?'

Katie smiled a knowing smile.

'I've got good news and bad news.'

'Let's hear it, then,' said Flutter.

'The bad news is that the left half, Tommy Rice, is no longer with us. He died three years ago in a car crash.'

'Oh, that's a shame.'

'The good news is that the other guy, Billy Spears, is still alive.'

'Great. Do you have an address?'

'I do. He lives with his daughter. I also have a telephone number.'

'Is he local?'

'He lives in a village called Felside.'

Flutter scratched his head.

'I don't think I know it,' he said. 'Is it far?'

Katie smiled.

'It's in Cumbria,' she said. 'I found it on a map. It's a few miles west of Kendal.'

'Kendal?'

'Where the mint cake comes from,' said Katie.

'Yes, I know where Kendal is, but that must be 300 miles away. It's not exactly a day trip, is it?'

'If we leave early and share the driving, we can easily do it in one day,' said Katie.

'We? You mean both of us?'

'Is that a problem?' she asked.

'No offence, but are you sure your old car will cope with the journey?'

'There's nothing wrong with my old car, but you needn't worry. I have access to a much better car.'

'You have?'

'The only reason I walk here most days is because it's only five minutes from home. I use my old car for running around locally because it's not worth getting the other car out of the garage.'

'I can't ask you to drive all the way up there,' said Flutter. 'I think I should go. Doris asked me to do her the favour. There's no need for you to drive at all. I could get a train.'

'There's no need for that,' said Katie. 'We're supposed to be a team, aren't we?'

'Well, yeah, but—'

'And whose the one with the interviewing skills and experience?'

'Well, I suppose, if you put it like that.'

'Why don't I call him and see if he'll talk to us first? Then we can argue about who will go up there, and how.'

'All right,' agreed Flutter. 'I'll get us a sandwich for lunch.'

Ten minutes later, Flutter walked back into the office, carrying two coffees and sandwiches.

'What are you doing tomorrow?' asked Katie.

'Tomorrow? Er, well, nothing, I suppose.'

'So, how about we go up to Felside tomorrow morning?'

This was an unexpected development and for a few moments, Flutter couldn't think what to say.

'I can always go on my own,' said Katie. 'I just thought, as you're so keen to go, you'd like to come along, too'

'What?' stammered Flutter. 'Yeah, that would be great.'

'You don't sound sure,' said Katie. 'You really don't have to come if you don't want to.'

'No, honestly, I'd love to come,' he said. 'It's just a bit short notice. I'll need to ask Doris if she can have Winston.'

'Good,' she said. 'I told Mr Spears we'd probably be there early afternoon. You call Doris, and I'll phone him back to confirm it.'

CHAPTER 13

Tuesday

When Katie had suggested they leave at 7 am, Flutter had raised no objections, but when his alarm went off at 6, his first thought was, why on earth had he agreed to get up so early?

He tried in vain to shake off his moody resentment, which he felt sure would sour the day, but it settled on his shoulders like a heavy cloud as he walked Winston to Doris's and it was still there as he waited outside the newspaper office. But then Katie pulled up and immediately his day filled with sunshine. He didn't know it, but he was about to begin a lifelong love affair, not with a woman, but with a car!

She wound the window down and leaned through.

'Good morning,' she said.

'Is this your car?'

'It was last time I looked.'

'A Range Rover?'

'You don't miss much, do you? Is there any reason I shouldn't have a Range Rover?'

Flutter laughed.

'I thought you were on the verge of going bankrupt.'

'It's not quite that bad. Anyway, this was my father's, so I didn't have to pay for it. It is expensive to run, though, which is why I rarely use it.'

'I've always wanted to drive one of these,' said Flutter.

She opened the door, slipped from the driver's seat and tossed him the keys.

'Well, there you go. It's your lucky day. You can drive this one.'

Flutter looked from the keys to the car, and then at Katie.

'Really? You don't mind?'

'As long as you're not a boy racer.'

'Ha! Fat chance. Most of the cars I've ever had would have struggled to keep up with the average snail.'

'Well, we're not racing snails today, so that won't be an issue. Besides, the alternative is I spend hours and hours behind the wheel. Yesterday you said I wouldn't have to drive, so now you can make sure I don't. We can change over if you get tired.'

Flutter climbed into the driver's seat while Katie climbed in next to him. He looked around him. He didn't think he'd ever seen so much leather and polished wood.

'This is amazing,' he said.

'It's just a car, and an old one at that,' she said. 'It might look posh, but it works just like any other car you've ever driven.'

'Oh, no,' he said. 'I promise you, I've driven nothing like this before.'

'Well, come on then, let's go,' said Katie. 'We've got a long journey ahead of us.'

Within five minutes, Flutter felt as if he'd been born to drive cars like this. It was like a dream come true and Katie seemed happy to let him drive without interfering, which made it even better.

'After you'd gone yesterday afternoon, I compared the handwriting on that original In Memoriam order with the funeral notice,' said Katie.'

'Is it the same writing?'

'Remember, there are fifty-odd years between when they were

written, and anything could have happened since then to affect how someone might write now.'

'I'm not expecting an expert witness statement, Katie. Just an opinion will do.'

'You're right, I'm not an expert, but I believe the same person could have written them.'

'Now that's interesting,' he said thoughtfully.

'Yes, it is, but I'm not sure how much it helps us.'

They reached Felside, a small village halfway between Kendal and Windermere, just after 2 pm. Being in a tourist area with a walking trail passing through it, there was sufficient trade to support two small shops, a post office, and a pub.

Flutter was pleased to find Katie was as hungry as he was. As she had provided the transport and had flatly refused his offer to pay for the fuel, he thought the least he could do was pay for lunch. While he was settling the bill, he asked the landlord if he knew a man called Billy Spears, or the Eldon family farm where he lived.

When he came back to their table, he had some news.

'The landlord says to get to the Eldon's farm we just need to follow the road out of the village and look for a narrow lane about half a mile away on the left. Then we just look for the first farmhouse along the lane.'

Katie looked at her watch.

'It's nearly 3 o'clock now. I told him early afternoon, so let's see what he can tell us.'

CHAPTER 14

BILLY SPEARS LIVED with his daughter and her husband on their farm. Apparently, they had brought him to live with them two years ago so they could look after him.

'He wasn't best pleased when we moved him up here,' the daughter explained. 'But he's not as fit as he used to be, and he needs looking after. He's not got full-blown dementia, but he has mood swings and his short-term memory can be rather hazy.'

'He will be okay talking to us?' asked Katie. 'We don't want to upset him.'

'Funny enough, his long-term memory is pretty good, and I'm sure he gets sick of us fussing around him so a change of company will probably do him good. Yesterday, when I told him you wanted to talk about his Army days, he was keen to meet you.

'Unfortunately, he's not in the best of moods today, but he said he's still willing to talk to you, although I can't promise for how long. I should warn you he will tell you when he's had enough, possibly rudely, but he means nothing by it, it's just how he is these days.'

She led them through to a room that looked out across a valley. In the distance, they could see an expanse of water that Flutter assumed must be Lake Windermere. An armchair stood before the large, wide window that looked out on the view, and they could just see the top of a head in the chair.

A tall, willowy man with dark eyes and a worried frown jumped up from the chair and turned to face them.

'Dad, these are the people who'd like to talk to you. Remember, I said they were coming?'

The frown vanished and the man's face broke into a smile.

'Of course I remember,' he said, reaching out to shake their hands. 'You're the people who want to talk about my Army days, isn't that right?'

'If you don't mind,' said Katie.

He pointed to two chairs placed alongside him.

'Come and sit down. I'd love to talk about the old days. They were some of the happiest days of my life.'

They sat down and couldn't help but find their eyes drawn to the view.

'That's quite a view,' said Katie.

'Yes, I suppose it is,' said Billy, then he leaned forward and lowered his voice, although his daughter-in-law had already left them to it. 'It is hard to believe but, if I'm honest, I find staring through that window all day gets boring.'

'Really?' said Katie.

'Since I came to live here, it's all I seem to do all day, every day,' he said. 'Believe me, it's one hell of a view, but there's only so much of it you can take. I'd like to go out more, but they won't let me go anywhere on my own in case I get lost. And they're busy on the farm and can't take me out, so I end up sitting here most of the time.'

Flutter thought he would die for a view like that from his window, but he could see Katie was striking up a rapport with Billy, so he kept quiet. If she could get him to relax and talk, that was just fine by him. Sure enough, it wasn't long before Katie had steered the conversation away from the view and Billy was reminiscing about his Army days and being posted to Malaysia with his mates.

Katie showed him the photograph.

'Do you recognise these lads?'

As Billy took the photo and studied it, his face broke into a smile.

'Privates Rice, Fulshaw, and Spears,' he said. 'The best halfbacks in the Regiment. That was taken just before the Queen's Cup final. We won 3-0!'

He pointed to each face in turn.

'That's Tommy Rice on the right, me in the middle, and Reggie on the left. The three musketeers we used to call ourselves. All for one and one for all, that was us.'

'A friend asked us to find out what happened to Reggie,' said Katie.

Billy sighed.

'Reggie was a lovely lad, but in a lot of ways he was very naïve. We were all kids, and not one of us was what you'd call a man of the world, but young Reggie didn't seem to know much about anything.'

'Did he struggle at school?' asked Katie.

'I didn't know him from school, but I think he must have because the poor bugger could barely read or write. Me and Tommy used to help him out when we could, but once the NCOs found out, they used it to humiliate him. Every two or three days, they'd ask him to read the daily orders out. They knew he couldn't do it, of course, but that gave them the excuse to laugh at him and tell him how stupid he was.'

'That wasn't fair,' said Katie.

'The bullying that went on was the one thing I didn't like about the Army. I reckon half the NCOs were psychopaths. They should have been locked away, not given free rein to bully people.'

'Tell us some more about Reggie. Is it true he had a girlfriend?'

A big smile lit up his face.

'Yes, that's right, he did. It was a surprise to all of us, but there was a girl back home in England who used to send him letters. He couldn't read them himself, so me and Tommy used to read them to him. Then he'd tell us what he wanted to say, and we'd write back for him.'

'You must have really liked him.'

'Everybody liked Reggie. He was just a sweet soul, you know. A boy like him should never have been in the Army. Trained killer? He couldn't have hurt a fly!'

Now his face fell, and for a moment Flutter thought he would burst into tears.

'I wish him and Tommy were here now,' he said. 'We lost touch after we got back from Malaysia.'

'Tommy died in a car crash,' said Katie.

'Did he? I didn't know that.'

'What about Reggie? We were told he died out in Malaysia. Is that right?' asked Katie.

Flutter watched Billy's face as it changed from shock to puzzled, and then resigned as he remembered.

'That's right, yes, he did. I'd almost forgotten about that.'

'Can you remember what happened?'

'He'd gone down to the village after hours. We all used to sneak out through this gap in the fence. We thought if we took turns and didn't all go at once, no-one would miss us. It seemed to work. We got away with it for months. And then, this one night, it was Reggie's turn to sneak out. We watched him head off through the gap as usual, and that was the last time we saw him. He never came back.'

'Why did he go into the village that night?'

'There were some beautiful girls in the village and he'd become friends with one of them.'

'Do you know her name?'

'Oh yes, I remember. Her name was Zarnie. We all knew her.'

'What about his girl in England?' asked Flutter.

'He didn't think she was serious about him. He liked her, but he felt she was too good for him and she would find someone better than him. She certainly wasn't like his village girl.'

He looked at them guiltily, then offered an explanation.

'The thing is, Reggie knew nothing about girls. All he'd ever done with his girl back home was hold hands and give her a peck on the cheek now and then. There were plenty of the girls in the village who offered a bit more excitement for a bit of cash, if you know what I mean?'

'You mean she was a prostitute? Is that why you said you all knew her?'

He nodded his head and sighed again.

'When Reggie first went to her, he'd never, well, you know. I think Zarnie knew that, and she was kind and patient with him. Well, that was it. He fell head over heels in love with her. I suppose we all did to tell the truth, but we all knew the score. Reggie couldn't see it, though. He thought him and Zarnie had something different. We thought he'd get over it, but he never did. He used to say he would marry her and take her back to England.'

'So what happened the night he died?'

'They told us it was bandits that killed him, but I don't think any of us really believed it.'

'Why not?'

'The officers used to tell us about the risk of meeting bandits at night, but it was just a story to make sure we always came back to camp on time. Everyone knew there weren't really any bandits in that area because the villagers told us there had been no bandits there for years. None of us would have gone out on our own if we thought there was a risk of meeting bandits. We might have been soldiers by name, but we were just kids having a bit of a lark. We certainly weren't looking to get killed.'

'If it wasn't bandits, what d'you think happened?'

'None of us really knows what happened because we weren't there. We only know what the Army told us. But no-one else ever encountered bandits while we were there, so why would Reggie?'

'Who found his body?'

'They didn't say, but the rumour was the chaplain found Reggie's body that very night.'

'The chaplain? What was he doing down there? Was he with a prostitute, too?'

Billy's nose wrinkled.

'I doubt it. The chaplain wasn't exactly a lady's man, if you know what I mean.'

'Why d'you say that?'

He pointed to the photograph, resting his finger just below Reggie's face.

'He was a pretty boy, Reggie. Looks like that can give certain people the wrong idea.'

'I'm not sure I follow. Are you saying you think he was gay?'

Billy sniffed.

'It wasn't called being gay in those days. Let's just say we thought he batted for the other side.'

'So, you're saying you think the chaplain was gay, and he fancied Reggie?' asked Flutter.

'There was never any proof, but the entire garrison thought the same as me. And he definitely showed an unhealthy interest in young Reggie.'

'You think something happened between Reggie and the chaplain?'

'All I know is that someone claimed to have seen the chaplain going through the fence that night not long after Reggie had gone. If that's true, it ties in with the rumour he found Reggie's body. But if the chaplain was there, and there were bandits around, how come they found Reggie, but they didn't find him?'

'Maybe it was his lucky night,' said Flutter.

'Or maybe it had nothing to do with luck, and there were never any bandits in the village on that night, or any other night. And there's another thing; the chaplain was gone within two days of Reggie's death.'

'Gone? What d'you mean gone?' asked Katie.

'Moved on. Re-posted. Call it what you like. I don't know about you, but I think that's odd. Just when all those young soldiers needed someone to help them cope with a mate's death, the one person whose supposed to be there for them was suddenly posted elsewhere. That can't be right, can it?'

'Did you ask why that happened?'

'Oh yes, we asked all right. But they told us the chaplain's posting back to England was a coincidence. It was already arranged and had nothing to do with what happened. End of story.'

'But you didn't believe it?'

'None of us believed it. If it was arranged beforehand, there would have been a new chaplain lined up to replace him, yet it was several weeks before one arrived. But you didn't dare challenge the official story in those days, so what could we do?'

Billy was becoming upset, and Flutter thought it was probably getting to the stage where they should stop. He glanced at Katie and could see she was thinking much the same.

'I'm sorry if this is upsetting you, Billy,' she said. 'Can I ask one more question, and then we'll go?'

He nodded.

'Can you remember the chaplain's name?'

Billy shifted awkwardly in his chair.

'No, I don't think I can, and I think you should clear off now.'

Katie looked at Flutter. He nodded his head. It appeared that was all the help they would get from Billy, so there was no point in upsetting him any further. They rose from their chairs.

'We're grateful for your help,' said Katie.

Billy said nothing and stared resolutely out at the view.

Flutter nodded towards the door. It was time to go.

They found Billy's daughter-in-law, made their apologies for upsetting him, and headed for the car.

'What d'you make of that, then?' asked Flutter, as he drove them away.

'How much credence should we place on the distant memories of a man with dementia?' asked Katie.

'I thought the memories of his Army days seemed quite clear.'

'Don't forget I had to remind him Reggie had died,' said Katie.

'I don't think that's important. It doesn't make his story any less credible, not to me at any rate. Are you saying you think he made it all up?'

'No, it's not that,' said Katie. 'The problem is, it's all based on rumours. There don't seem to be any hard facts. And even if there were any, how do we prove something that happened halfway around the world, sixty years ago?'

She sighed as she remembered what Robbie Bright had said.

'Robbie told me even Doctor Who would struggle to find out what happened sixty years ago in a faraway land. Maybe he had a point.'

'Chin up, Katie,' said Flutter. 'We don't need Dr Who. This is where your brilliant investigating skills come into their own. Trust me, you'll be able to join all the dots, and solve the case like a young Miss Marple. With a bit of help from yours truly, of course.'

'You don't want to believe everything you see on TV. And, anyway, in case you've forgotten, neither of us actually is a detective.'

'Yes, but then, nor was Miss Marple. Anyway, you've done a fair bit of investigating, haven't you?'

'Poking around in the recent past isn't quite the same thing. And you do know Miss Marple's not real, don't you?'

Flutter cast her a sideways look.

'I'm wondering what's happened to the Katie I met a few weeks ago.'

'What's that supposed to mean?'

'The Katie I first met was up for a challenge. She was willing to help a bloke she'd never met before. She even stood by him when a gangster turned up.'

'And your point is?'

'My point is you're not exactly overflowing with enthusiasm or determination right now, are you?'

'I didn't say I'd given up. I'm just saying we're at a disadvantage because we're not professionals, and we don't exactly have a lot to go on. Out of the three names we have, one was the victim, one is dead, and the one who is alive could only offer a heavily prejudiced suggestion of what he thinks might have happened.'

Flutter smiled.

'You noticed he didn't like the chaplain, did you?'

'I think he made it quite clear he doesn't like anyone gay, don't you?'

'Even so, d'you think there might be something in this gay chaplain idea?'

'Anything's possible, isn't it?'

'But how can we check the guy out if we don't have a name? You said yourself we're unlikely to get any information from the Army, especially if there's a scandal involved.'

'I could try my great-uncle again.'

'D'you think he'll help? What about his loyalty to the regiment?'

'He'll be reluctant, but you never know,' said Katie thoughtfully. 'Perhaps I just need to find the right way to approach the subject, so he doesn't think I'm asking him to betray anyone.'

CHAPTER 15

As he drove, Flutter had a nagging feeling there was something different about the car, and it was worrying him. He thought perhaps it was the state of the lane they were on, but when he turned onto the main road, the car didn't feel any better. If anything, it was getting worse. They had reached the pub now, and he turned off the road into the car park and stopped.

'Where are you going?' asked Katie.

'We need to stop a minute,' he said. 'Something doesn't feel right.'

He jumped out and walked around to the back of the car. He thought he knew what he was looking for and, sure enough, the rear tyre on the passenger side looked ominously flat.

Flutter sighed.

'Bollocks!' he muttered. 'Now I'll have to change the wheel, which means I'll end up getting filthy.'

Katie's window opened, and she leaned out.

'What's up?'

Flutter pointed at the tyre.

'We've got a puncture.'

'Oh, no, that's just my luck.'

'Where's the spare wheel on this thing?'

'Underneath, at the back. Lift the floor in the boot, take the jack out and undo the nut-thing to lower the wheel to the ground. D'you want some help?'

'No, you're all right. There's no point in both of us getting dirty. Sit tight. This shouldn't take too long.'

He opened the boot, raised the floor and lifted the jack out to reveal the "nut-thing" as Katie called it. He used the wheel brace to lower the spare wheel to the ground, then took the jack from the boot, loosened the wheel nuts and jacked up the car. As he had expected, he got filthy removing the wheel, but at least it wasn't too much of a struggle.

He dragged the spare wheel from under the car and stood it up so he could roll it along. Then he uttered a four letter word he wouldn't normally use.

'What's the matter?' called Katie from the car.

'When was the last time you had a puncture?'

'Oh, it was months ago. Flat as a pancake. I was in the car park in the middle of town. A nice man changed it for me.'

'What did he do with the flat tyre?'

'He put it back where the spare came from, and he told me to make sure I... Oh, damn!'

'He told you to get it repaired, and you forgot, right?'

'I was on the way home and in a hurry. The car stayed in the garage and I didn't use it for a couple of weeks. I completely forgot about the puncture.'

He studied her face. There was no doubt she was feeling guilty, and his mood immediately softened.

'I suppose it could have been worse,' he said. 'At least the tyre didn't burst while we were doing seventy miles an hour on the motorway.'

'I'm so sorry.'

'Don't get upset. No-one died, did they? Okay, so I got dirty. It'll wash off.'

'What do we do now?'

'Well, we can't drive home with a flat tyre, but at least the pub's open. We'd better ask the landlord if he knows a good mechanic, or a tyre fitter. You'll have to call them, though. I've lost my phone.'

'When did you lose it?'

'I'm not sure. I haven't seen it for days. It'll be at home somewhere, I expect.'

'You should have said. I could have called and then, when it rings, you'll know where it is.'

'That's not going to be much help up here, is it?'

'When we get back, then,' said Katie. 'Right now, you need to get cleaned up. I'll speak to the landlord.'

It didn't take too long for Flutter to wash his hands, but there wasn't much else he could do without a change of clothes.

A gloomy-looking Katie was perched on a stool waiting for him at the bar.

'I hope you're not in a hurry to get back,' she said.

'My diary was empty last time I checked, and Doris is looking after Winston, so any time tonight will do for me.'

'I don't think that's going to happen. It looks like we're stuck here until tomorrow morning.'

'Oh, right. Well, like I said, I've got nothing to rush back for. You?'

'I've got nothing arranged, but that's hardly the point, is it? I don't want to sleep in the car!'

'This place does bed-and-breakfast. Perhaps they've got two rooms for tonight.'

'You'll be lucky at this short notice.'

'I'll ask the landlord when he comes back behind the bar.'

Katie excused herself and went off to the ladies.

The landlord had been wandering the room collecting empty glasses, but now he returned to his position behind the bar.

'Any luck?' he asked.

'They say they can't get here until tomorrow morning,' said Flutter.

'You can leave the car where it is,' he said helpfully. 'It'll be safe enough.'

'I don't suppose you've got any rooms vacant?'

'Let me have a look.'

The landlord pulled a ledger from under the bar and thumbed through it until he found the page he was looking for.

'You're in luck,' he said. 'We've had a cancellation, so there's an empty double.'

'Is that all you have?'

'Like I said, we've had a cancellation or there wouldn't be anything.'

'Right, we'll take it,' said Flutter.

The landlord found a pen.

'If I can just have your name,' he said.

'Gamble,' said Flutter.

In a very slow, deliberate hand, the landlord wrote in his book. As if to reassure himself, he spoke the names out loud as he wrote.

'Mister, and Missus, Gamble,' he said. 'One night, bed-and-breakfast.'

Flutter thought about explaining that he and Katie weren't actually married, or even in a relationship, but it had been a long day and, frankly, he was feeling too weary to care.

'That'll be eighty pounds, please.'

'Eighty? For one night?'

'This is a very popular spot with passing walkers,' said the Landlord. 'Of course, you don't have to take the room. If you don't want it, I'm sure someone else will take it.'

Flutter sighed as he reached into his pocket for his wallet and reluctantly counted out the cash. The landlord handed him his receipt just as Katie came back, then he reached under the bar again and produced a key.

'Here you are, Mrs Gamble,' he said. 'It's room number 6.

Through that door over there, up the stairs, turn left, and it's first on the right.'

He placed the key on the bar and wandered off to collect more empty glasses.

Katie's mouth had dropped open, but before she could say anything, Flutter grabbed the key, took her arm and led her away from the bar.

'Mrs Gamble?' she hissed. 'What the hell's that all about?'

'We're sharing a room,' he said.

'Over my dead body,' she said.

'I've paid for it now, and it's the only room they have.'

'But I don't want to share a room. I hardly know you.'

Flutter sighed.

'I was just trying to find us somewhere better to sleep than the car.'

'And I'm not pretending to be Mrs Gamble.'

'I'm not asking you to pretend to be anything. And anyway, that wasn't my idea. The landlord asked for my name and then put Mr & Mrs in the book. I couldn't be arsed to argue because I'm tired, and I didn't think it mattered.'

'Well, it damned well matters to me!'

'Okay, fine,' said Flutter. 'If it matters that much, ask him to change the names in his book. I thought you'd be grateful to have somewhere comfortable to sleep, but obviously I was wrong. If it's really such a big deal, I'll sleep in the room, and you can sleep in the car.'

She glared at him, and her jaw jutted forward.

'I don't want to sleep in the car.'

'Which is precisely why I paid for us to have the only empty room in the village.'

'It'll be cold and uncomfortable in the car.'

'Well, don't look at me,' said Flutter. 'I was happy to roll up my sleeves and get filthy changing a wheel so we could drive home, but

I'm not prepared to sleep in the car. It's not my fault you didn't get your tyre repaired last time you had a puncture.'

He could see she had a retort on the tip of her tongue, but he knew he'd scored a winner with that last comment. She knew it, too, and kept her reply to herself.

'For God's sake,' said Flutter in exasperation. 'I thought I was doing you a favour. It's not as if I'm asking you to climb into bed with me.'

She glared at him.

'I should damned well hope not. If I find out you planned this—'

'Oh, come on, Katie, get real! Are you seriously suggesting I arranged a puncture? And how could I have known the spare wheel was flat? I didn't even know you owned this car until this morning!'

He could see she didn't have an answer for this, but he also knew she also was unlikely to back down in a hurry.

'If you're hoping there will be any funny business…'

'I promise you, there's no danger of that happening.'

'What's that supposed to mean?'

Now it looked as though he'd offended her, and not for the first time in his life, Flutter wondered if he would ever understand women. The comment probably hadn't come out quite the way he had intended, and he really didn't want to offend her, but he felt he had done absolutely nothing wrong, and he was damned if he would apologise. He ignored her question and pointed to the door that led to the stairs.

'At least let's look at the room,' he said. 'Maybe it will have two beds.'

Reluctantly, she led the way to the room, unlocked the door, and led him inside. It was a large room with a double bed, two armchairs, and a small ensuite shower room. A window looked out across the main road and over the fields beyond.

'There you go,' said Flutter. 'You can have the bed. I'll push the two armchairs together.'

'I'm smaller than you. I'll have the armchairs.'

'I can't let you do that,' said Flutter.

'It's my fault we're stuck here.'

'Yes, it is, but you didn't do it on purpose, and it changes nothing.'

'Look, I don't expect special treatment just because I'm a woman.'

'It's not because you're a woman.'

Her face told him she didn't believe him.

'I'm not going to keep on arguing with you,' he said. 'I'm sleeping in the chairs, and that's it. We can share them if you insist, but it seems crazy when there will be an empty bed.'

'You mean it, don't you?'

'I'm sorry if you don't like it, but I can assure you I would make the same offer if you were a bloke.'

A wicked smile creased her face.

'You'd offer to share the armchairs with another man?'

'Well, I don't know about that, but I'd offer to let him have the bed.'

He could see she was wavering, and her mood had definitely improved.

'So, come on then, it's make your mind up time.' he said. 'What are you going to do? Share the room with me, or sleep in the car?'

'I already told you I'm not sleeping in the car.'

'That's settled, then,' said Flutter. 'We're sharing the room.'

He looked at his watch.

'It's 5 o'clock. I don't know about you, but I'm not hungry yet. I could do with a shower, though. But if that will be a problem...'

'Why don't I go for a walk while you have a shower? I'll give you half an hour. When I come back, you can go for a walk while I have a shower.'

'Okay, I can work with that.'

He looked down at his grubby clothes.

'I wish I had a change of clothes.'

'We passed one or two shops on the way through the village. If this is on a hiking trail, there must be a shop that sells hiking gear. I'll have a look while I'm out.'

. . .

Half an hour later, Katie returned carrying a large bag which she emptied onto the bed, then she noticed his face and stopped.

'What's the matter?'

'I've just remembered I'm on probation.'

'So, don't commit any crimes and you'll be fine.'

'No, it's not that. I'm not supposed to spend a night away from home without telling my supervisor.'

'Are you wearing a tracking device?'

'No, of course not.'

'Do you have to check in with her before you go to bed?'

'Now you're being ridiculous.'

'My point is she won't know where you are, will she?'

'No, I suppose not. I didn't think of that.'

'Or perhaps you think I'm going to tell her?'

'And why would you do that?'

'Exactly. And if she did somehow find out, I can vouch for the fact it wasn't planned, and I'm sure the landlord would verify what's happened.'

Flutter sighed. He didn't look convinced.

'Look,' said Katie. 'I understand you don't want to step out of line, but it's not as if you did it on purpose, is it? It's my fault we're stuck here, and I promise I'll make sure they know that if it comes to it. I'm sure they'd take such a mitigating factor into consideration.'

'Yeah. I suppose you're right,' admitted Flutter. 'Anyway, there's not much point in worrying about it when I can't change it, is there?'

He managed a smile and nodded towards Katie's bag.

'What have you got in there, then?'

'I found a shop,' she said. 'They had toothbrushes and toothpaste. I also got you a tee shirt, but I had to guess at the size. You can take it back if it's too small.'

She passed him the tee shirt, and he pulled it on. It fitted perfectly.

'Wow, thanks. How much do I owe you?'

'After you paid for the room? I don't think so. They've also got jeans and hiking trousers, but I wasn't sure what you'd want. They're open until 7 pm if you want to look.'

Flutter knew a hint when he heard one.

'I'll have a look while you're in the shower. I'd better call Doris, and let her know she's dog-sitting overnight.'

'She won't mind, will she?'

'No, but I don't like to take her for granted.'

CHAPTER 16

AFTER THEIR INITIAL disagreement about sharing the room, "Mr and Mrs Gamble" seemed to have reached a pact. It turned out Katie was much less concerned about her privacy than she had made out, and hadn't batted an eyelid when Flutter came back to find her drying her hair dressed in nothing but a damp towel.

Not sure where to look, and not wanting to risk starting another argument, he had gone to the window and stared out across the fields, even resisting the temptation to look over his shoulder when she announced she was about to turn her back on him to get dressed.

They had gone down to the bar shortly after 7 pm, intending to have a meal and then go back to their room and sleep. But it turned out a small band was playing in the bar that night, and by the time they had eaten the place was packed to the rafters with a mix of locals and hikers staying at a hostel in the village. A good time was being had by all and it was unlikely they would get any sleep with the noise of the band...

It was well after 11pm by the time the band finished playing and the bar emptied, and with more drinks inside them than either had intended, Flutter and Katie were now getting on famously.

Katie finished her drink and placed her glass down on the bar.

'I suppose we ought to get some sleep.'

'Yeah, I guess you're right,' said Flutter. 'It's been a good night, though, hasn't it?'

'Yes, I've really enjoyed myself. It must be the company.'

Flutter looked around the room. There were just a handful of people left now.

'Yeah, they're a good crowd, aren't they?' he said.

'That wasn't quite what I meant,' she said.

Flutter didn't reply, and when she looked at him, he was staring at her, puzzled.

'I meant you, you idiot,' she said. 'You're good company.'

'Am I? I'm just being me.'

'Well, I suggest you keep on being you.'

'If we're exchanging compliments,' he said, 'I should tell you I can't remember the last time I enjoyed myself so much.'

She smiled.

'I can't believe that. I'm sure you've plenty of girlfriends who are more fun than me.'

'Girlfriends? Oh, no, not me. I'm off women.'

'Oh, wait,' she said. 'Would this have anything to do with the thing you said you'd tell me about when you knew me better?'

Flutter nodded.

'Yeah, something like that,' he said.

'D'you think you know me well enough now?' she asked.

'What?'

'Do you want to talk about it? It's obviously bothering you, and I think it's stopping you from enjoying yourself. Getting it out in the open might help.'

'I dunno. It's not something I'm proud of.'

'Maybe you're just looking at it the wrong way. Come on, let's go upstairs and talk.'

She slipped from her barstool, and Flutter dutifully followed.

When they reached the door to the stairs, he stepped forward and held it open for her.

'You're quite the gentleman, aren't you?'

'That depends on your point of view,' he said. 'There are plenty of women these days who think it's an insult to hold a door open for them. I was taught it's good manners to hold a door open for someone else, no matter who they are. I can't see how my good manners demeans anyone, but what do I know?'

He followed her up the stairs and into their room.

She sat on the bed and patted the covers next to her.

'Come and tell Katie all about it,' she said.

Flutter suddenly felt very nervous. She was flirting and, while he couldn't deny he found her attractive, he also couldn't forget the fuss she had made earlier about sharing a room. This was a dilemma he'd rather not have to deal with.

'I'm not sure that's a good idea,' he said.

'Nothing will happen,' she said.

'I think I'll sit in an armchair, if you don't mind.'

She pouted and smiled.

Definitely flirting, he thought.

'Just look upon me as your big sister.'

Flutter settled himself in an armchair.

'I should warn you I don't have a big sister, and if I had one, I don't think she would flirt with me.'

She broke into an even bigger smile.

'All right, think of me as a good friend. We are friends, aren't we?'

'Are you going to listen to me, or keep on teasing me?' he asked. 'I know I said I'm off women for now, but I'm not a monk.'

She made a big show of putting on a straight face and sat up straight.

'Right,' she said. 'Message understood. So, tell me about it.'

'I was going to be married,' he said.

'When was this?' she asked.

'Six years ago.'

'What happened?'

'It sounds naïve, I know,' he said, 'but I thought she wanted to wait until we got married before we slept together. It turns out I thought wrong.'

'She was cheating?'

Flutter nodded.

'It turned out she had been doing it for over a year. What made it even worse was that she was shagging one of my best mates. He would probably have been my choice for best man. Best man my arse!'

Katie was struggling to think what she could say that wouldn't sound cliched, but for the moment she had nothing to offer.

'Ah,' she said. 'I see.'

'Then, to top it off, I found out everyone knew but me. Everywhere I went I could feel people watching me, laughing at me, and I realised they'd probably been doing that all along.'

'I'm sure they weren't.'

'Sure they were. I was a fool, and they all knew it.'

'What did you do?'

'Quit my job, and moved away.'

'I thought you said you've never had a proper job?'

'It was nothing special, just driving.'

'Where did you move to?'

'I didn't go far. I was still in London but in a place that big you don't have to go far to move away and start over.'

'And now I suppose you think every woman will cheat on you?' asked Katie.

'Something like that, yeah.'

'Have you dated anyone since?'

'I've had a few one-night stands, but nothing serious.'

'Have you talked about this with anyone before?'

'No. You're the first. I normally keep it to myself.'

'D'you want my opinion?'

Flutter shrugged. He wasn't sure what he wanted.

'For what it's worth, I think you were far too young to marry, and you had a lucky escape. Painful as it must have been, imagine how much worse it would have been if she had married you and it was still going on when you found out?'

'Yeah, I worked that one out for myself. The problem is, it's a trust thing, isn't it? How will I ever know if I can trust another woman?'

Katie sat up straighter.

'Hang on,' she said. 'You can't assume that just because she cheated on you, that means we're all the same.'

'Yeah, but how will I know?'

'When someone jumps out of an aeroplane, they trust their parachute will work, don't they?'

'Right. But where does using a parachute come into it?'

'Because it's about trust. The parachutist knows that parachutes have sometimes failed to work, but trusts it won't happen to them. They take that leap knowing that the chances of the parachute failing are so slim the risk is acceptable.'

'That's easy for you to say.'

'Is it? If I looked at things the way you do, we wouldn't be here now.'

'I'm not with you.'

'It would be like me saying because one man has raped a woman that means all men are rapists, therefore you must be one, and consequently I'm in grave danger right now.'

'That's a bit extreme. You're not in any danger.'

'Yes, it is extreme, but my point is you can't apply the same rule to everyone based on one experience. If everyone dropped out of the game, the first time it broke their heart, we would all stay single for ever!'

'I don't know if I can go through that again.'

'D'you think you're the only one who ever chose the wrong partner? Look at me; I thought I'd married Mr Perfect, but it turned out he was the biggest bastard you could meet. Yes, it hurt, but that doesn't stop me from trusting other men will be different.'

'I get that, but the reality is I'm scared it will happen again, you know?' said Flutter.

Katie's smile had disappeared. She studied his face for a moment and then seemed to decide.

'Is this excuse just for my benefit?' she asked.

'Sorry?'

'If you don't find me attractive, just say so. I'm big enough to deal with rejection. You don't have to invent a story to soften the blow.'

Flutter was confused.

'Hang on,' he said. 'Is this some sort of test?'

'Test? What do you mean, test?'

'Well, if it's not a test, I must have missed part of the conversation. Have we just gone fast-forward for a few minutes?'

'What?'

'One minute I'm telling you about my problem and now, suddenly, it's all about you feeling rejected because I don't find you attractive. Now, I know for a fact that I didn't say I don't find you attractive, so when did that happen?'

'But you wouldn't even sit next to me.'

'Katie, I think you're clever and gorgeous, and I really like you, but I think you're only flirting with me because you've had a drink or two. If we slept together tonight, you'd probably regret it in the morning, and then where would we be? Besides, you've got Robbie back at home.'

'Robbie and I are finished. We are no longer an item.'

'Oh, really? I'm sorry.'

'We'll, I'm not. I'm glad. Robbie's a pig.'

'Wait a minute. So you're on the rebound. Is sleeping with me going to be some sort of revenge on him because you know he doesn't like me?'

Katie jumped to her feet, her eyes wide, her face red.

'No, I'm not on the bloody rebound, and I'm not out for revenge. Anyway, what makes you think I want to sleep with you? D'you really think I'm that easy?'

'All right, Katie, take a deep breath, calm down, and sit down,' said Flutter.

She looked as if she'd like to strangle him, but she took a couple of deep breaths and then sank back on to the bed. There was a stony silence for a couple of minutes.

'I'm sorry,' she said, eventually. 'I don't know what came over me.'

'Jesus, Katie. Do you know how confusing this is?' asked Flutter. 'One minute you're moaning because you think I don't find you attractive, and now I've said I do find you attractive, you think I'm saying you're easy. You're the one who started flirting! What is it you're trying to prove?'

'If you're off women, as you say, who was that woman I saw you with in the coffee shop?'

Flutter was slow to make the connection.

'What woman?'

'Last Monday afternoon you said you were going to the dentist, but I saw you in Leslie's having coffee with a rather good looking woman.'

Flutter grinned.

'Have you been following me?'

'No, I have not. I was going to get myself a coffee. As far as I was aware, you had gone to the dentist, but there you were, drooling over some woman.'

Flutter was enjoying himself now.

'You're jealous,' he said. 'Is that why you've been flirting with me?'

'Don't be ridiculous.'

'Why are you so interested in who she is?'

'Because you couldn't take your eyes off her.'

'How do you know? I had my back to the window.'

'Yes, but there's a mirror on the wall. I was looking straight at you, but you were so focused on her you didn't see me looking through the window.'

'Ha! So, you are jealous.'

'I don't know who she is, and I'm curious, that's all. '

'You're being nosey,' said Flutter.

'You can call it that if you want,' said Katie. 'I would say I'm looking out for you.'

'But you do know who she is. You've even spoken to her. She's my probation supervisor.'

Katie looked suspicious.

'That was her?'

'It was our first meeting.'

'Isn't it unusual to meet in a coffee shop?'

'She said their offices are being refurbished, and she wanted our first meeting to be informal, to make it easier for me. Sort of break me in gently.'

'It sounds odd if you ask me,' said Katie. 'I'm glad your meeting on Thursday was a bit more formal. How did it go, by the way? I didn't like to ask, and you never mentioned it.'

'She called me when I was on the way to say the decorators were still there and the offices couldn't be used.'

'This gets more unprofessional by the minute. Is the entire probation service run in this haphazard fashion, or is it just a local shambles?'

'Don't ask me,' said Flutter. 'Believe it or not, I've never dealt with them before.'

'Where is this office, anyway?'

'It's on Queen Street. I can't remember the number. I've got her card at home.'

'I thought I knew all the offices on Queen Street, but I don't recall a probation office.'

'Well, that's what the card says,' said Flutter wearily.

'So when is your next meeting?'

'We met on Saturday.'

'Is it normal, meeting on a Saturday?'

'She had to come and check out my house, so we had a meeting there.'

'She came to your house? On a Saturday? Is that usual?'

'It was her idea, not mine. She said it was easier than trying to make time during the week and it would kill two birds with one stone.'

'As Alice said, this is becoming curiouser and curiouser,' said Katie.

'Who is Alice?'

'Alice in Wonderland,' said Katie. 'It means something sounds weird.'

'Yeah, well, it's even more weird for me.'

'I mean it, Flutter. I admit I don't know much about the probation service, but I can't believe this is how it's supposed to work.'

'I admit it's not quite what I was expecting, but if I piss her off, she could give me a hard time. For now, I'm just trying to go with the flow and not rock the boat. I want to keep her sweet, at least until I can see how the land lies.'

'Well, you might be happy to go along with it, but it doesn't sound right to me,' said Katie.

Flutter had been stifling a yawn for a few minutes, but now it got the better of him.

'Sorry,' he said. He looked at his wristwatch. 'Blimey, it's gone one o'clock. Can we carry on this conversation in the morning?'

'No need to apologise,' said Katie. 'I'm tired, too. It's been a long day for both of us. We should get some sleep.'

'I'll just push these armchairs together,' said Flutter. 'And I'm sure I saw a spare blanket in the wardrobe.'

'I've been thinking about that,' said Katie. 'I think you should sleep on the bed.'

'I'm not letting you sleep in those chairs,' said Flutter.

'It's an enormous bed. I'll sleep in it, and you can sleep on it,' said Katie. 'If we each keep to our own side, it'll be fine.'

'Are you sure?' asked Flutter.
'I think I can trust you,' she said.
Flutter grinned.
'Yeah, but the thing is, can I trust you?'
He ducked as a pillow flew over his head.

CHAPTER 17

WEDNESDAY

Although there was a sheet and blanket between them, Katie had made sure she kept them as far apart as possible when they climbed into their separate parts of the bed, and insisted they sleep facing away from each other.

Even so, Flutter had been painfully aware of her presence, and her slow, rhythmic breathing was a constant reminder of just how close she was. The very idea that he could accidentally roll towards her in his sleep, and that she could misinterpret his intentions, had made it impossible for him to relax. As a result, he had only slept in fits and starts.

Katie, however, seemed to have no such concerns and had fallen asleep almost as soon as her head hit the pillow. As Flutter lay awake, he considered how he felt about that. His first thought was that it was because of the effects of the drinks she had consumed earlier. He knew from experience just how easy it was to fall asleep after a few beers.

The longer he thought about it, though, the more unfair he felt it was that he had had just as much to drink, yet he couldn't sleep at all!

He eventually found consolation in the theory that perhaps it had nothing to do with drink and was actually a sign that she trusted him.

For a while, this idea made him feel inordinately pleased, but this only seemed to make sleep even more difficult to achieve. At one stage, Flutter thought he had dreamt a cockerel was crowing, only to realise it was 5 am, and he wasn't dreaming at all. But then exhaustion finally got the better of him and he slowly drifted off to sleep, despite his concerns.

It was now 7:30 and Flutter was slowly coming round. For the first few seconds, as he lay on his back, his mind seemingly reluctant to clear, he did not know where he was. His left arm seemed to be pinned down and something was draped across his chest. Then he realised there was something else draped across his legs. And now, something was tickling his nose.

Instinctively, he reached up with his right hand and swept the hair off his face. Hang on a minute, he thought. How can there be hair on my face? My hair's not that long!

Slowly, he moved his hand down from his face. Something round and hairy was resting on his chest, just beneath his chin. Carefully, he felt his way around the object and, as he realised what it was, he almost cried out. Despite the layers between them, somehow, while Flutter had been asleep, Katie had turned over and flung an arm across his chest and a leg across his legs, and was now snuggled up to him, with her head resting on his chest.

At first he was horrified at the idea of trying to explain this away. After all, she had made it perfectly clear last night how she felt about the situation. But then he slowly realised he didn't have any explaining to do. After all, he wasn't the one who had rolled over and snuggled up to her. It wasn't his arm, and his leg, draped across her, was it?

It took a while to ease his slightly numb left arm from underneath her, but eventually it was free, and he slipped it around her shoulders, careful to keep the blanket and sheet between them. To his surprise, he suddenly felt very protective of her, but then he was fond of her, so it was only natural, wasn't it?

Now he had asked himself the question, he wondered if feeling protective was a good thing, or would it complicate their working relationship? Then he decided he would worry about that some other time. For now, he was going to lie there and let Katie sleep until she woke up. He knew she had enough worries to stop her sleeping well at home, so, if using him as a pillow helped her sleep, that was fine by him.

Half an hour later, Katie began to stir. She wasn't one of those bright, sparkly, jump out of bed full of the joys of spring people, and was what might best be described as a slow burner first thing in the morning. It took her a few minutes to notice her surroundings, but as she did, she became increasingly alarmed.

At first she had wondered why her pillow was so hard, and it had taken a couple of minutes for her to work it out. Now she realised that, as far as she could make out, she was draped across Flutter, with her head on his chest and with his arm wrapped around her. How on earth this had happened?

Her first thought was that she had been mistaken in her belief that he could be trusted, and that he had been trying to take advantage of the situation. But if that was the case, why were the blankets and sheets still between them, and why were they both on his side of the bed?

Cautiously, she took his hand and lifted his arm away. Then, she carefully, and slowly, raised her head and rolled back over to her own side of the bed. All the time she kept a watchful eye on Flutter, but he seemed to be fast asleep and didn't stir, so she silently slipped from the bed and headed for the bathroom.

Once he heard the click of the bathroom door closing, Flutter opened his eyes. He was sure, by the way she had stiffened as she woke up, that Katie had been shocked to find how they were laying.

He had been expecting this, but the fact she had slipped out of bed so quietly suggested she had realised she had been the one to roll over, and she was hoping he had been asleep and unaware of what had happened.

This was the sort of situation where the devil in Flutter would normally insist on teasing and embarrassing his sleeping partner, but this was Katie, and Katie was different. If she wanted to pretend it hadn't happened, that was okay by him because, much as she might deny it had happened, she couldn't take away how right it had felt with his arm around her as she slept.

The tyre fitter would not be there until 10:00, so after breakfast the Landlord suggested they might go for a walk.

'You can't come all the way up here and not take in the scenery, even if it's only for an hour or two,' he said. 'There's a pleasant walk along the river. It would be a shame to miss it. If you leave me the car keys, I can see to the tyre fitter when he arrives.'

Katie thought this sounded like a good idea, and Flutter wasn't going to argue with her, so they set off through the village as directed.

They soon found the path and followed it alongside the river, which, because it had rained little recently, was more of a gentle, meandering stream than the raging torrent the Landlord had suggested. At one point the river fed a pond, which was home to a handful of swans and ducks, before it wandered off into the distance, finally disappearing around the side of a distant hill.

The path branched off around the pond at this point and, after a short debate, they wandered around the pond before heading back to the pub.

'I once spent an entire afternoon by the river in Waterbury, trying to count the ducks to impress a girl,' said Flutter as they ambled around the pond.

'Really? That must have been a headache. How many were there?'

'I don't know. I gave up when I got to 237. The little buggers wouldn't stand still, so I probably counted most of them more than once.'

'That was very inconsiderate of them, not standing still for you.'

'Yeah. I kept asking, but they wouldn't take any notice.'

Katie smiled.

'Exactly how old were you when you tried this?'

'It was a long time ago. I was a teenager.'

Flutter lapsed into silent reminiscence, and Katie wondered if perhaps she would have to prompt him, but then he suddenly spoke.

'I thought she was the girl of my dreams,' he said.

'And you thought you could impress her by counting ducks?'

Flutter smiled.

'I know. It sounds daft now, doesn't it? But it seemed a good idea at the time.'

'When was this, exactly?'

'Fifteen, sixteen years ago.'

'Wow! You were young. Was she your first girlfriend?'

'First serious one, yeah.'

'Don't we all think our first love is the one?' she asked. 'I know I did. Mind you, I thought the same when I met my ex-husband, and I was completely wrong about him!'

'She was lovely,' said Flutter. 'Nice looking and slim, and she had these lovely long, shapely legs. Small up top, but I didn't mind that.'

'My. How very chivalrous of you,' said Katie sarcastically.

'I didn't mean it like that. I mean, I know now, sometimes less is more, right? But I was young back then. She was the first girl I ever... well, you know. '

'So, what happened?'

'I was an idiot. When I met her, I was sixteen years old. I had dropped out of school, with no idea what I wanted to do with my life. I suppose you could say I was a bit of a lost soul, but then she came along and suddenly everything changed. For the first time in my life, I felt as if I had something to look forward to. I even enrolled in college to carry on where I left off at school and get some qualifications.'

'I sense there's a, "but", coming up,' said Katie. 'So, what happened?'

'A girl in my tutor group at college took a shine to me. We were doing the same course, and she always seemed to end up sitting next to me. It soon became obvious she fancied me. The thing was, she had these enormous boobs. Well, I'd seen nothing like it before, and she knew I was curious. And she was no innocent. She was what my aunty used to call "all tits and no knickers" and she knew exactly what to do to feed my curiosity...'

'Ah! So, you ditched the legs for the boobs?'

'I was drawn like a moth to a candle. I guess it was what you'd call a fatal fascination.'

'How did your girlfriend find out?'

'I could probably have got away with it if I'd kept quiet, but I felt so bad about cheating on her my conscience got the better of me. I told her I didn't want to go out with her anymore. Broke her heart, it did.'

'I see. So, you're a boob man, are you?'

'What I am is a bloody fool. It turns out "Boobs on legs" just wanted one thing, and once she got that, I was history.'

'What happened after that?'

'I tried to make it right with my ex.'

'Broken trust is just about impossible to repair.'

'Yeah, don't I know it,' said Flutter bitterly. 'She got her own back, though.'

'Who did?'

'Jenn—,' Flutter stopped himself mid-word, and hurriedly tried to correct himself. 'The girl with the legs.'

Katie stopped dead.

'Hang on a minute. Did you say, Jenny?'

Flutter kept walking, forcing her to keep up or get left behind. She kept up.

'No.'

'You were going to, and then you corrected yourself.'

'You must have misheard,' he said.

'I don't think so, do you?' said Katie, scenting a story. 'So let me get this right. You had a girlfriend called Jenny when you were a teenager, and now you've come back to Waterbury, you have a probation supervisor with the same name. Isn't that a bit of a coincidence?'

'Not really. I should imagine there are hundreds of Jennys in England.'

'And that same Jenny came to visit your house on a Saturday? No wonder she was so possessive of you.'

'Was she?' asked Flutter, before adding hurriedly, 'I wouldn't know about that. Anyway, I'd know if it was the same Jenny, and I'm telling you, it isn't.'

Not for the first time that morning, she studied his face, trying to discern the truth, but once again, he was a blank canvas offering no clues to help her.

'Okay,' she said suspiciously. 'If you say so, it must be so.'

'Anyway, the other Jenny and I were a long time ago, and this one says she's happily married.'

'That's what she told you?'

'Yes.'

'That seems a bit of an odd topic for her to be discussing with you. Do all probation supervisors discuss their personal lives with their charges?'

'I wouldn't know. I've never met one before,' said Flutter, innocently.

'You said this girlfriend got her own back. How did she do that?'

'She started going out with me again and let me rent a small flat so we could live together. Then, when I'd spent every penny I had, to get the flat just how she wanted it, instead of moving in, she told me it was all over. The whole thing had been a ploy to set me up for a fall.'

'Ouch! That must have hurt.'

'Yeah, you could say that.'

'Is that why you went to London?'

'It was like the beginning of the end. It didn't help that I bumped into her mum a few days later. She told me it was all my fault, and I wouldn't be able to spot a good thing if it slapped me around the face. As if I hadn't already worked that one out for myself.'

'But you must have had lots of girlfriends since then, haven't you?'

'Apart from the one I told you about last night?'

'She can't have been the only one. There must have been ten years between the two.'

'I had the odd casual relationship, and a few one-night stands, but nothing serious.'

'You don't look the sort who'd be lonely for long.'

'I didn't say I was lonely. As I said, I have occasional girlfriends, but I always make sure they understand I'm not looking for a long-term relationship. If I think they're getting serious, I end it.'

'And that's your plan for the rest of your life, is it?'

'I don't bother trying to make plans. I find they always seem to go pear-shaped, and end in disappointment.'

They had walked all the way around the pond, and were now on the main path, heading back to the village and the pub.

'It can't be that bad,' she said.

'You think? Don't forget, I've just come out of prison. I mean, that wasn't part of my plan, now was it? That was someone else's plan.'

'Yes, I see what you mean. But it hasn't all been like that, has it?'

'I actually thought things might be looking up when I found out I'd inherited the big house. But then there was always this nagging doubt in the back of my mind, like it was all too good to be true, and you were there yourself when that went pear-shaped.'

They walked in silence for a minute or two.

'I want to apologise for this morning,' said Katie.

'Apologise for what this morning?'

'For putting my arm across you in my sleep.'

Flutter had been wondering if this conversation would happen.

'Did you?'

'You know very well I did. I know you were trying to avoid embarrassing me, but I'm afraid you're not very good at pretending to be asleep.'

'Ah. So you want to apologise for cuddling up to me?'

'I wasn't cuddling up to you.'

'I think you'll find you were. You had your leg draped over me as well.'

Katie's face began to redden.

'Yes, well, it was an accident, and I'm sorry.'

'I'm not,' said Flutter. 'I haven't been that close to a woman in ages.'

'I'm not sure how I'm supposed to take that,' said Katie.

'You can read creepy stuff into it if you want,' said Flutter. 'But before you do, perhaps you should ask yourself this: did you sleep well?'

'Well, yes, I did.'

'Better than you do at home?'

'Yes.'

'But you still have all the same worries that normally keep you awake, right?'

'And your point is?'

'Well, perhaps you slept better because you felt secure.'

'Secure? You mean sharing a bed with a man I've only known a matter of weeks?'

'We might have shared a bed, but we didn't actually share a bed, did we?'

'I suppose not, if you put it like that. So what's your point?'

'Could it be that you slept like a log because you felt safe and secure? Safe enough that you even felt you could cuddle up to me?'

Katie stared at Flutter.

'You're kidding,' she said.

'Why not?' he said. 'You told me the other day that you lay awake at night worrying, and yet one night next to me, and you sleep like a log!'

Katie laughed.

'Look, if it makes you happy to think I slept like a baby because you were there to protect me, that's fine by me, but I think you may be reading too much into it. I think I slept so well because of all that booze we drank.'

'I had as much to drink as you did, and it didn't make me sleep.'

'So, sleeping next to me didn't make you feel secure, then?'

Flutter thought it was probably better if he avoided mentioning how he'd been feeling lying next to her and steered the conversation in another direction.

'The thing is, you don't need to apologise, because I wasn't the least bit offended,' he said.

'Come to think of it,' said Katie. 'How come you spared my blushes? That's not like you, is it?'

'I dunno what you mean.'

'I get the feeling you'd enjoy embarrassing someone in that situation, wouldn't you?'

'I'd tease a bit, but I'm not into humiliating people in public.'

'Yet you didn't tease me. Why is that?'

'I'm sure you can work that one out for yourself,' he said.

Katie hadn't expected that for an answer. It stumped her for a minute, and she wondered if he was playing games, or was he feeling as confused as she was?

'There is one thing, though,' she said. 'Robbie must never know we shared a room.'

'I thought you and him were finished.'

'Yes, we are.'

'So, it's none of his business what you've been doing.'

'Yes, I know all that, but I'd just rather he didn't know.'

'He only speaks to me when he has to, so I'm not likely to bring it up in conversation, am I?'

'Just promise me you won't tell him.'

'Okay. I promise I won't tell him. Anyway, it's not as if anything happened, is it?'

'I know that, but if he finds out we were away all night, he'll put two and two together and say we arranged it.'

'It's a relationship built on trust then, you and Robbie?'

'I told you, there is no relationship.'

'But you're still worried about what he'll think. To me, that suggests you think it may not be over.'

'Look, I don't want to fall out with you because of an idiot like Robbie, so can we talk about something else?'

'Okay,' said Flutter. 'Whatever you say.'

CHAPTER 18

THURSDAY

Even though they were sure a funeral would not be taking place, Flutter and Katie had agreed to meet outside Waterbury cemetery at 10:15. Flutter looked at his watch for the umpteenth time. It was 10:20. Katie was late, and Flutter was getting irritated.

If this had been a date, Flutter wouldn't have worried. After all, wasn't it the lady's privilege to be late? But this wasn't a date, it was a stakeout. They knew there was a strong possibility they were on a fool's errand, but if someone had placed the notice in the newspaper for a reason, this was the obvious place to test that theory.

To make matters worse, it had been raining for the last two hours, and a dirty grey sky suggested it would not stop anytime soon. Flutter had a good enough coat, but with neither hat, nor umbrella, a steady trickle of cold rainwater had run down his neck while he had been waiting, and it was doing nothing to improve his mood.

As he waited outside the gate, a man and woman approached the gates. As he stepped aside to let them pass, the woman nodded her head and offered a half smile. They were huddling under an umbrella; the man stooped and apparently much older. He seemed to need her help and, with his left arm linked with her right, she was hurrying him along. As she hastened the old man through the gate into the cemetery, the walking stick in his right hand dragged uselessly along the ground.

Flutter felt it was obvious he was struggling to keep up and wondered if the woman was rushing him because of the rain. Or perhaps she found his slowness irritating and didn't care he was finding it difficult. Either way, it seemed unfair to the poor old guy. He thought about calling out to them, but then quickly forgot his concern as someone took his arm.

'Sorry I'm late,' said Katie. 'I got held up…'

'Don't worry,' he said, his irritation forgotten. 'It's not 10:30 yet.'

She looked him up and down.

'You look half-drowned. You'd better come under my umbrella.'

'Are you sure you don't mind me being so close?'

She grinned up at him.

'After Tuesday night, I think I can trust you not to think of it as an invitation to go any further.'

She was a good six inches shorter, and Flutter had to duck his head to get under the umbrella. Once there, he leaned awkwardly towards her, not sure where to put his hands.

'Wouldn't it be a lot easier, and a lot more comfortable, if you put your arm around me?'

'Er, well, yeah. I suppose it would,' he said, uncertainly.

He threaded an arm around her and she raised the umbrella high enough for him to stand up straight.

'It'll be a suitable cover, won't it?' suggested Katie. 'We'll look as if we're out for a romantic stroll in the rain.'

Flutter took this as his cue. He had something he wanted to get off his chest.

'About Tuesday night—'

'Look,' interrupted Katie. 'We had a good time, didn't we?'

'Best time I've had in ages, to be honest,' he said.

'And, best of all, we did nothing either of us would regret.'

'Would you regret it?' he asked. 'I'm not sure I would.'

He said it without thinking and immediately wished he hadn't, as he felt her body stiffen. It was only for the briefest of moments before she relaxed again, leaving Flutter uncertain if he'd said the wrong thing.

'The point is, our working relationship hasn't changed,' she said noncommittally.

Flutter felt she had avoided the question, but at least she didn't appear to have been offended by his comment. He also wasn't sure he completely agreed with her assessment of their relationship, but quickly decided this was probably one of those occasions when he should keep his opinion to himself.

'I've decided it would be best if Robbie didn't know anything about us going to Cumbria.'

'I'm not with you.'

'What he doesn't know about, he can't twist into something to get jealous about.'

'As I said before, me and him aren't exactly bosom buddies exchanging gossip every five minutes. And if he really does twist things like you say, you'd be better off without him.'

'I don't want a lecture. I just want you to promise you won't tell him.'

'I already promised, didn't I?' said Flutter. 'But if it makes you happy, I'll promise again, okay?'

'Thank you,' said Katie.

'D'you think the rain will change things here?' he asked, keen to change the subject.

'Who can say? We don't know for sure that anything will happen, do we? I suggest we hang around until 11 o'clock. If nothing's happened, I think it's safe to say we're wasting our time.'

'Are we going to stand here by the gate? I think we should take a walk down to the far end nearer Reggie's grave.'

'You're right,' said Katie. 'He seems to be the centre of whatever's going on, so I think that's probably where we should focus our attention.'

They walked through the gates and began retracing the route they had taken before, but this time, they knew where they were heading. About a hundred yards ahead, the old couple Flutter had seen earlier were nearing the far end of the central path.

'There's someone ahead of us,' said Katie.

'It's just some old couple. I saw them earlier.'

'An old couple? How old?'

'Didn't take that much notice. She was about 70, I think. I got the impression he was a few years older, but I didn't really get a good look at him.'

'They're going in the same direction as us.'

'There aren't that many paths to choose from, are there? To get anywhere in this cemetery, you have to use this central path.'

'Where do you think they're going?'

'Visiting a grave, I should think.'

'In this weather?'

Flutter hadn't considered this, but now Katie had pointed it out...

The couple ahead had reached the end of the path, and now they turned right.

'Shit,' muttered Flutter.

'Are you thinking what I'm thinking?' asked Katie

'Come on,' said Flutter, ducking from under the umbrella and breaking into a trot. 'Let's get a move on.'

Because of the rain, Katie had dispensed with her normal heels in favour of knee-length boots, but she knew she would struggle to run fast enough to keep up with him.

'You go on,' she called. 'I'll only slow you down.'

It was just a hunch, and if he was wrong, he would look an idiot, but Flutter began to run, eyes fixed firmly on the couple ahead. He could see they had almost reached the corner where the Cypress tree watched over Reggie's grave.

The old man seemed reluctant to go any further, and the woman turned briefly in Flutter's direction as if to check if she was being followed. Suspicion confirmed, she turned back to the old man, shouted something at him and began urging him on towards the tree.

As Flutter reached the end of the main path and turned right, the couple reached the tree, and now the woman let go of her charge and took a few paces away. As she did, the tiny figure of a second woman stepped from behind the tree and approached the old man, pointing an accusing finger at him. She was saying something to him, but even though he was closing the distance fast, Flutter couldn't hear what was being said.

The small woman then joined the first woman under the umbrella and watched impassively as the old man let go of his walking stick, clutched at his chest and, as if in slow motion, sank to his knees, and then fell forward in a crumpled heap.

Flutter instinctively knew the old man was having a heart attack and, ignoring the two women, he rushed to the old man's side and rolled him on his back. He felt for a pulse, but there was nothing there. He turned to the two women.

'Call for an ambulance!'

'We don't have a phone.'

Flutter fumbled through his coat, looking for his own phone.

'It's all right, I've got mine,' shouted Katie. Still a good few yards away, she had seen the old man collapse and knew what she needed to do.

Flutter aimed a disgusted look at the two women as he returned his attention to the heart attack victim. Then he administered CPR, which he continued, with Katie's help, for another fifteen minutes until the paramedics arrived.

CHAPTER 19

Sadly, despite the combined efforts of Katie, Flutter, and the two paramedics, the old man was beyond help and was pronounced dead on arrival at the hospital. In the meantime, the rain had stopped, and the police had arrived in the shape of DS Robbie Bright and two uniformed PCs.

Bright ignored Katie and Flutter and first spoke to the two women. After a few minutes, he instructed the two PCs to drive the women to the hospital. Then he walked over to Flutter and Katie and listened to their version of events.

'So, let me get this straight, Flipper,' said Bright when they'd finished speaking. 'You think you've just witnessed a murder, and I should have arrested those two sweet old ladies, is that it?'

'Exactly,' said Flutter, refusing to be rattled by Bright deliberately getting his name wrong.

'The fact is, you're lucky the man's wife doesn't want to press charges,' said Bright.

'What?'

'Maybe he would have survived if you'd waited for the paramedics instead of playing at doctors.'

'I wasn't playing at anything,' said Flutter. 'The guy needed CPR and I provided it.'

'What qualifies an idiot like you to know when to do CPR?' sneered Bright.

'If you must know, I did a first aid course when I was inside, and I passed with flying colours.'

Katie was furious with Bright.

'The ambulance took fifteen minutes to get here. I suppose you would have left the poor man lying there in the rain, would you?' she demanded.

'Well, no, of course not.'

'So, don't try to be clever,' she said. 'We did our best to save a dying man in the pouring rain, and all you want to do is try to score cheap points. What's the matter with you?'

'The point is, you could have made him worse.'

'The guy had no pulse,' said Flutter. 'That means he was dead. How could we make him worse than that? How would that work? Anyway, why have you let those two women go? They set the old guy up and frightened him to death. I saw it with my own eyes.'

'I'm not going to waste my time arresting two old ladies for being out in the rain when I've got real, serious crimes to solve.'

'Out in the rain? You should arrest them for murder. That's serious enough, isn't it? How is that going to be a waste of time?'

'What you're saying is total bollocks,' said Bright. 'There is no murder. What you saw was a man who has suffered for years with chronic angina, finally succumb to his condition.'

'Yes,' said Flutter. 'But only because his wife had him almost running all the way down here and then, as if that wasn't enough to kill him, the other woman jumped out and frightened the crap out of him.'

'I'll bet you anything you like a postmortem would say he died of natural causes,' said Bright, hoping that was going to be an end to it.

But he was wrong. Flutter had no intention of letting it go so easily.

'Listen. Katie's told you the story behind all this. The old bloke was a chaplain in the Army. A chaplain killed Reggie Fulshaw over a Malaysian woman called Zarnie. I bet the woman you let go was called Zarnie, wasn't she?'

Bright said nothing, but Flutter was sure he was right.

'I thought so. Don't you think it's all a bit of a coincidence?'

'What I think is that your involvement in this story has clouded your judgement and you have misinterpreted what you saw.'

'What's that supposed to mean?' demanded Katie.

'I believe you saw what you wanted to see.'

'Are you suggesting we're making it all up?' asked Flutter.

'I'm not saying that, but do you have proof any of this historical stuff is fact?'

'Well, no,' said Flutter.

'You must know what the Army is like,' said Katie. 'They won't tell anyone anything.'

'Exactly,' said Bright. 'So you have no conclusive proof the dead man killed this young soldier all those years ago. In fact, you don't even know for sure if the boy was murdered. And even if you had proof, what difference does it make now? In case you didn't know, we can't charge a corpse with murder!'

'Yes, but those two women know the truth. They also knew the old guy was dying, and they just stood there watching.'

'They told me they didn't want to get in the way while you were trying to resuscitate him. That sounds quite reasonable to me.'

'But they did nothing to help him.'

'It may surprise you, but the vast majority of people have no idea how to give CPR, so what else should they have done?'

'But I saw—'

'You saw a woman point a finger at a man. I think you'll find that's an everyday occurrence for a lot of men. If we arrested every woman who pointed her finger at a man, we'd have no room in the cells for real criminals.'

'But his wife was rushing him along. He was almost running, trying to keep up.'

'Of course she was hurrying him along. It was pissing down with rain and he's a sick man. Would you have been hanging around so he could get soaked? Or course not.'

'If he was that sick, she shouldn't have brought him out in this weather, and she shouldn't have been making him run.'

'She says he wanted to go for a walk. He enjoys walking in the rain.'

'There's a vast difference between a walk and what she was making him do,' said Flutter. 'Besides, it was clearly an ambush. The second woman was waiting behind a tree!'

'You saw it as an ambush, because that's what you wanted to see,' said Bright. 'She says she was sheltering from the rain.'

'But what about Katie? She saw the same as me.'

'She saw the old man fall to the ground, and she saw you rush to help him but, by her own admission, she was struggling to keep up with you and didn't see exactly what happened before he collapsed.'

'This is bollocks,' said Flutter. 'Why won't you take this seriously?'

'I'm afraid the only thing that's bollocks is your murder theory.'

'What about the fake funeral notice?' asked Katie.

'I think I told you before, it's not a crime.'

Bright's patience was running out and his face was turning distinctly dark, but Flutter didn't care.

'But it all adds up. Are you really so stupid you can't see it?'

Bright studied Flutter's face for a moment before he answered.

'If you were a properly trained detective, and weren't just playing games, you might understand that first, you actually need proof a crime has taken place. Then you need solid evidence of guilt before you even think about accusing people. So, even if I was to take your supposed case seriously, I can't build a murder case based on remote possibilities suggested by a convicted criminal.'

'Oh, now I get it,' said Flutter. 'You don't want to know because it's me, is that it?'

'Have you ever heard the expression, "when in a hole, stop digging"?' asked Bright.

Flutter looked confused, but Bright didn't wait for an answer.

'I'm going now, Flipper,' he said. 'I've got actual crimes to solve, but if I were you I'd take heed of my warning.'

He started walking towards his car. Flutter wanted to keep arguing, but when he looked at Katie, she was shaking her head.

'Leave it,' she warned him.

'What was that stuff about digging a hole?' he asked.

'He means you need to know when to stop arguing.'

'So, what happens now? Are we supposed to leave it at that?'

'I think you should go home and cool down,' said Katie.

'What are you going to do?'

'Well, I'm a journalist and a man died here this morning. I'm going to see if I can find those two ladies at the hospital and get their side of the story. I'll catch up with you later.'

CHAPTER 20

It was late afternoon when Katie arrived at Flutter's house. He led her through to the kitchen and put the kettle on.

'Have you cooled down now?' she asked.

'Yeah, I'm sorry. I just got a bit frustrated by his attitude. I know he's your boyfriend, but he can be a real pain in the arse.'

'I told you he's not my boyfriend anymore.'

'Yeah, well, if you say so,' said Flutter doubtfully. 'Whatever. I'm sorry I got stroppy.'

'There's nothing wrong with having a bit of passion about your cause,' said Katie. 'But there's a time and a place to show it. Arguing with someone like Robbie Bright when he's already made up his mind is a waste of time.'

'Yeah, you're right. Reading people isn't one of my superpowers,' he admitted.

Katie smiled.

'That's not really something a detective should own up to,' she said.

'Yeah. Well, maybe Bright was right. I'm not exactly over-qualified to be a detective, am I?'

'Then it's just as well you've got me by your side, isn't it?'

As Flutter made two mugs of tea, he asked her what had happened at the hospital.

'The old man was the Reverend Franklin, and he was officially pronounced dead when he arrived at the hospital.'

'We already knew he was dead,' said Flutter. 'You didn't need a medical degree to know that.'

'No, but you need one to declare him officially dead.'

'Fair enough. What about the two women?'

'You mean Mrs Franklin, and Yasmin.'

'Yasmin? I thought her name was Zarnie.'

'We got that bit wrong, I'm afraid.'

'What does that mean?'

'It means the story isn't as simple as we thought.'

Flutter sighed.

'I'm not doing very well, am I? I've pissed off Bright, and got the story all wrong, without really trying.'

'Self pity isn't the most attractive attribute,' said Katie with a smile. 'Actually, I think you're doing fine, but you need to accept I'm the one with the experience and you're still learning. Perhaps you need to reign in your confidence a bit, and let me ask the questions until you're more experienced. Do you think you can do that?'

'Do I have a choice?'

'If you want us to work as a team, I think it's the way it has to be.'

'You drive a hard bargain, don't you?'

She smiled again.

'Every time,' she said.

'Okay, I'll do it.'

'Good. Now, would you like to know what really happened to Reginald Fulshaw?'

He handed her a mug of tea and pointed to the lounge.

'Follow me. It's more comfy in there.'

'What Billy told us was correct, almost,' began Katie as she followed him. 'Reggie did fall for one of the village girls—'

'The prostitute, Zarnie, right? So who was the woman at the cemetery?'

'That's what I'm trying to tell you. Zarnie was a prostitute, but she wasn't Reggie's girlfriend and she wasn't the woman at the cemetery.'

'But Bright said she was Zarnie.'

'Actually, he didn't say her name. You assumed you were right because he said nothing. The woman we saw at the cemetery was Zarnie's sister, Yasmin. Reggie used to go to the village to see Yasmin, not Zarnie.'

'So why did Billy tell us—'

'I don't know. Maybe he got it wrong, or perhaps Reggie let his mates believe it because he didn't want them to know he was still a virgin.'

Flutter was doubtful, but there again, if he had still been a virgin at twenty himself, would he have told everyone? No way!

'Okay, so he went to see Yasmin. What difference does it make?'

'It makes all the difference in the world. It was because the chaplain, Franklin, believed Reggie was infatuated with a prostitute that he followed him into the village the night he died.'

'So Franklin wasn't gay?'

'Not according to his wife. She says he told her he wanted to persuade Reggie he was making a big mistake. He thought if he caught him red-handed, Reggie couldn't deny the relationship. In the event, Franklin caught someone else with Zarnie.'

'Ah. That would have been awkward,' said Flutter.

'We don't know who that someone was, but we do know he didn't take kindly to being interrupted, and a fight ensued. Reggie came to the Chaplain's rescue but ended up getting his head bashed in for his trouble.'

'Blimey! So he was in the wrong place at the wrong time?'

'Exactly. He died trying to save the Chaplain.'

'So he was a hero?'

'I would say so.'

'Then why was he buried in secret? Didn't Franklin come forward and explain?'

'Maybe in different circumstances he would have, but this was the Army, remember? Can you imagine the scandal if it had ever come out that an Army chaplain had been in a fight over a prostitute?'

'Would it be such a big deal?'

'Maybe not these days, but this was sixty years ago, and things were different back then. They couldn't possibly allow a scandal like that to come out. They had the reputation of the Regiment to think about.'

'So, there was a cover-up?'

Katie nodded.

'Exactly. Someone came up with the story about bandits, and they quietly returned the chaplain to England, with a warning that he was never to tell anyone what had happened.'

'And he kept his mouth shut all those years? Christ, what a bloody coward!'

'Apparently the Church knew, but there were strong ties with the Regiment. Franklin had regular reminders to keep his mouth shut or lose his job.'

'So whose idea was it to bury Reggie in secret?'

'They gave Franklin that job. He felt he had no choice but to do what they told him or become the centre of the scandal if it ever came out.'

'So who placed all the In Memoriam notices?'

'Mrs Franklin.'

'His wife? Why did she do that?'

'When they suddenly found themselves removed from the Army and back in a tiny parish in England, Franklin told his wife he had found Reggie dead that night but forgot to mention he caused his death.'

'But she found out, right?'

'At first she thought Franklin had been hard done by, but then five years later Yasmin wrote to her, explaining what had really happened and how she had learned from other soldiers how everything had been hushed up. She had loved Reggie and wanted to know why he wasn't honoured as a hero.'

'I can understand that,' said Flutter. 'So what did Mrs Franklin do?'

'Now she knew the truth she felt her husband had made a fool of her and wanted to make him pay. That's when she came up with the idea of punishing him by reminding him every year in the local newspaper.'

'For sixty years? Bloody hell, that's not punishment, that's torture.'

'Anyway, she and Yasmin kept in touch over the years and eventually Yasmin saved enough money to come over and see Reggie's resting place.'

'So they hatched a plan to kill him. I knew it.'

'Yasmin just wanted to see Reggie's grave. She had arranged to meet Mrs Franklin but did not know Franklin was going to be there; that was Mrs Franklin's idea. But when Yasmin saw him, she couldn't ignore him.'

'And the shock killed him. I can't say I'm surprised.'

'Yes, maybe, but Yasmin's only guilty of loving Reggie. She didn't kill Franklin.'

'Maybe not, but Mrs Franklin isn't exactly squeaky clean, is she?' Katie nodded her head.

'She definitely doesn't regret her husband's death, that's for sure.'

'So, what happens now?'

'Yasmin goes back to Malaysia, and Mrs. Franklin stays at home.'

'So, basically, she's taken sixty years to kill him. She's got away with a very slow murder.'

'I very much doubt you could prove that,' said Katie. 'Especially if a post mortem says it was natural causes. And, as Robbie said, with his history of angina, it's more or less a foregone conclusion.'

'So, Reggie's killer got away with it, and we don't have the faintest idea who it was. Does that mean we failed?'

'I don't think you should see it like that. We always knew it was going to be a long shot. At least we know what happened. Perhaps you need to accept that you win some, and you lose some.'

Flutter nodded his head slowly.

'Yes, I suppose you're right,' he said. 'But what are we going to tell Alma?'

'We could tell her the truth.'

'I dunno about that. I don't want her to think Reggie had been cheating on her.'

'But didn't you tell me she met her husband before she knew Reggie had died?'

'Yeah, but what difference does that make?'

'Doesn't it suggest she had already accepted it was over between her and Reggie?'

'I hadn't thought of it like that.'

'Or, you could tell her Reggie died trying to help someone, that there was a scandal, but he wasn't involved in it.'

'You mean, like he was collateral damage?'

'Something like that, yes.'

'And not mention Yasmin at all? Is that the right thing to do?'

'I suppose you could call it lying by omission,' said Katie. 'But Reggie's long gone, and Alma will be gone soon, too. Does she really need to know about Yasmin?'

'Hmm. Let her die in peace, you mean.'

'What she doesn't know about, she won't worry about,' said Katie.

'Yeah, I think you're right. That's what I'll tell her.'

CHAPTER 21

FRIDAY

It was just before 8 am, and Flutter was just about ready to take Winston to the park, when the doorbell rang. Flutter wondered who would call this early, but before he could open the door, someone pounded upon it and a familiar voice began shouting out.

'Police! Open the door!'

It was Robbie Bright.

Flutter opened the door with a big smile on his face.

'Sergeant Bright! How nice it is to see you again. Unfortunately, I'm just going out.'

Bright offered the suggestion of a smile in return.

'Oh, no, you're not, Flipper. You're staying right here. We have a search warrant.'

He shoved a folded sheet of paper into Flutter's hand as he barged past.

'I want a thorough search,' he bellowed to the half a dozen uniformed police officers and single detective following in his wake. 'Every cupboard, every drawer, under the mattress. You know the drill.'

The uniformed officers were led by PC Blackwell. He had

history with Flutter and looked immensely pleased with himself as he stomped past Flutter into the kitchen, flexing his fingers in anticipation as he snapped on a pair of latex gloves.

'Mind my dog,' shouted Flutter. 'I'll hold you responsible if anything happens to him.'

'He's asleep,' called Blackwell. 'He won't even know I've been here.'

'Have you done any laundry in the last couple of days?' asked Bright.

'Laundry?'

'Come on, Flipper. You know what laundry is. Have you washed any clothes in the last couple of days?'

'No,' said Flutter. 'It's in the basket upstairs. And if you think deliberately getting my name wrong is going to wind me up, you're wasting your time.'

Bright raised his voice again.

'I want everything in the laundry basket bagged and tagged,' he called up the stairs.

'There's a lot of you to search a small house,' said Flutter. 'What are you expecting to find?'

'I believe—'

Before he could finish, there was a loud crash from the kitchen. Flutter ran to see what had happened. The kitchen looked as though a pack of gremlins had run wild. All the drawers had been tipped out on the floor, the contents of the cupboards had been added to the pile, and then, in a final flourish, Blackwell had dropped an armful of plates.

'Oh, bloody hell,' said Flutter, as a smiling Bright peered over his shoulder.

'Oh dear,' said Bright. 'Tut, tut, Constable Blackwell. You really should be more careful.'

An evil grin spread across Blackwell's face.

'Whoops, sorry,' he said. 'How clumsy of me. It's all right, though. The dog's still fast asleep.'

More sounds were coming from upstairs as the team systematically trashed the house. Flutter could see where this was going, but he knew there was nothing he could do about it.

'Going somewhere nice, were you?' asked Bright.

'I was going to take my dog for a walk, drop him with his dog sitter, and then go to work.'

Bright sucked on his teeth.

'Somehow, I don't think that's going to happen,' he said.

'Look, what's this about?' asked Flutter. 'If it's because of what happened yesterday, I accept I was wrong and I shouldn't have said some of the things I said. I'm happy to apologise, if that's what you want.'

'You really are an idiot, aren't you?' said Bright. 'Do you really think I'd go to all his trouble, just because a tit like you called me a few names? That might be the sort of petty revenge that appeals to you, but I'm an adult; I can rise above that sort of crap.'

Now Flutter was becoming concerned.

'Well, if it's not that, why are you here?'

'If you'd like to cast your tiny mind back to yesterday, I said I had a real, serious crime to deal with.'

'Yeah, and?'

'And that's why we're here. I suppose you're going to tell me you know nothing about it.'

'Too bloody right I am,' said Flutter. 'Whatever you think I've done, you're barking up the wrong tree.'

'And I suppose you're also going to tell me you've not been associating with any known criminals since you were released?'

Flutter's mind was racing. Strictly speaking, this was true. He had been associating with a London gangster called Jimmy Jewle, but not by choice. The fact is, Jewle was the last person Flutter wanted in his life, but if he tried to explain, would Bright understand? Of course not. He wasn't here to empathise with Flutter and his bad luck.

'I dunno what you're talking about.'

'Oh, I think you do,' said Bright. 'You've been associating with a known criminal called Bennet, and I know it's a fact because we've had a tip off.'

Flutter breathed a sigh of relief. Bennet was his uncle, and while he knew some of his uncle's business activities could be described as shady, as far as Flutter was aware, he had never actually been arrested or convicted of a crime. Bright was new to the area, and obviously not yet au fait with all the local villains.

'Bennet is my uncle. I was trying to find out who my real father was, and it turns out Bennet knew because my dad was his brother. What was I supposed to do, ignore the one man who could tell me what I wanted to know? As far as I'm aware, he's not a criminal, and there was nothing criminal about our meetings, it was just family business.'

'Are you sure he didn't ask you to do a little job for him?'

'No, he didn't.'

The PCs had finished searching the house and were gathering by the front door.

'Found anything?' asked Bright.

'Nothing,' said Blackwell, who seemed to be their spokesman.

'I told you I had nothing to hide,' said Flutter. 'And is it really necessary to break everything? Can't you be a bit more careful?'

'You can make a complaint if you're not happy,' said Blackwell.

'Don't worry, I will,' said Flutter. 'Now, can you take your elephants away so I can clean up this mess?'

Bright smiled.

'We haven't finished yet,' he said, fishing a second search warrant from his pocket. 'This is for your other house. I hear it's bigger. Lots more hiding places for us to search.'

'It's not my house.'

'It's registered in your name.'

'Yeah, but I don't live there.'

'Why not?'

'Because I don't like it. I'm getting rid of it.'

'Of course you are,' said Bright, doubtfully. 'But the fact remains, you still own it, and it's still a potential hiding place. I'd like you to come with us while we carry out our search.'

Blackwell stepped forward to grab Flutter, but he backed away, out of reach.

'Hang on a minute,' he said. 'What about my dog?'

'Your dog?' asked Bright.

'Look, I can see what's going on here. I'm being stitched up again, aren't I?'

'I don't know what you mean,' said Bright. 'We're just following a line of enquiry.'

'Yeah, right,' said Flutter. 'See, the thing is, I was stitched up like this last time, so I know how it works.'

'How's that, then?' asked Bright.

'You're going to cart me off now, and I'm not going to step back out of that police station for days, if at all.'

'I can't deny it's a possibility if we find what we're looking for,' said Bright.

'He's stalling,' said Blackwell. 'Why don't I just drag him out so we can get on?'

'I'm not stalling,' said Flutter. 'I just want to make sure my dog won't be left here to starve.'

'What do you suggest?' asked Bright.

'Let me call the dog sitter so she can come and collect him.'

Bright smirked.

'You must think I was born yesterday if you think I'm going to let you make a phone call. You could just as easily being telling someone to hide the evidence.'

'There is no evidence to hide,' said Flutter.

'Yes, well, we'll see about that when we get there,' said Bright. 'If we ever get away from here.'

'All right,' said Flutter. 'I'll give you the number, and you call her.'

'Who me?'

'It doesn't matter who makes the call as long as someone does. I'm not leaving until I know my dog's going to be looked after. So, you can sort the dog out, and I'll come quietly, or I can go kicking and screaming. Your choice.'

Bright sighed.

'Okay. Blackwell, make the call,' he said.

'Are you serious?' asked Blackwell. 'All this fuss for a dog? Why don't you let me cuff him and drag him out so we can stop wasting time?'

'Tell me, Blackwell, have you been promoted in the last five minutes?' asked Bright.

'You what?' said Blackwell.

'So, you're still PC Blackwell, then?'

'Of course I am.'

'And you understand I'm Detective Sergeant Bright?'

'Course.'

'Right. Now we've established who is in charge here, perhaps you'd be good enough to carry out my orders, and make the phone call.'

'I wasn't trying t—'

'Yes, I think you'll find you were,' said Bright. 'Now, just make the bloody call. We don't want to give the animal rights mob an excuse to complain, do we?'

Flutter fished in his pocket for his mobile phone, then remembered he had lost it, but he knew Doris's number off by heart, so it didn't matter.

'Where's your mobile phone?' asked Bright. 'We're going to need to take that as well.'

'Lost it,' said Flutter. 'I haven't seen it for days.'

'That's very convenient,' said Bright.

'I hardly ever use it, so I don't miss it,' said Flutter.

'I meant it's very convenient you've lost it right now, just as we want to take it,' said Bright.

'What is it I'm supposed to have done?' asked Flutter. 'Committed a murder?'

Bright's face darkened, and he leaned in close to Flutter's face.

'This isn't bloody funny,' he snarled.

'Do I look amused?'

Bright grabbed the front of Flutter's sweater and marched him outside, where he pinned him up against the wall. A uniformed head popped out to see what was going on.

'It's okay,' said Bright. 'I'm just getting him out of your way.'

The head popped back in again, and Bright turned back to Flutter.

'Now listen up,' he hissed. 'A man has been attacked and is currently lying in a coma in the hospital. The chances are he will never recover, so we're looking at attempted murder, and you are our number one suspect. This means you are in deep shit and yet you seem to think this is some sort of game.'

Flutter couldn't believe his ears.

'Attacked? Who? I haven't attacked anyone. I've never even been in a fight.'

'Is that right,' said Bright. 'Only that's not what I've heard.'

'What's that supposed to mean?'

'All in good time,' said Bright.

Just at that moment, PC Blackwell emerged from the house.

'She reckons it'll be about half an hour before she can get here to collect the dog.'

'Oh, good,' said Bright. 'In that case, DC Brennan can lead the troops down to Willow Grove.'

He nodded to the other detective, who took it as a sign to lead the others back to their cars for the journey across town.

'What about my dog sitter?' asked Flutter. 'How's she going to get in and collect the dog if there's no-one here?'

'That won't be a problem,' said Bright. 'You and me can have a chat while we wait for her. Come on, let's go inside.'

He nodded towards the front door, and Flutter led him back inside.

'When your dog's gone, you can come down to the station with me. My boss would like to have a little chat.'

'What if I don't feel like coming down to the station for a chat with your boss?'

Bright offered the faintest of smiles.

'Then you'll give me an excuse to beat the crap out of you for resisting arrest.'

'You'd like that, wouldn't you?' said Flutter.

'It's up to you whether I need to use force.'

'Yeah, right,' said Flutter. 'The reality is you're just as bad as that thug Blackwell, aren't you? Katie tells me you're different, but you're not, are you?'

'I don't think a man in your position should be comparing me to a neanderthal like Blackwell.'

'Who else would I compare you to if you're going to behave like him?'

'And of course, you're squeaky clean, are you?'

'I don't go around beating people up, if that's what you mean.'

'I think a jury will be the judge of that,' said Bright.

The inference was obvious enough, but it went straight over Flutter's head. He was much too busy trying to score points.

'You were happy enough to let the cave dweller smash up my kitchen, weren't you?' he said. 'You even thought it was funny. What's Katie going to think when I tell her about that?'

Bright shifted uncomfortably and looked distinctly embarrassed.

'If I was like Blackwell, I wouldn't have arranged for the dog sitter to come and collect your dog.'

'I'll give you half a brownie point for that,' said Flutter. 'But it doesn't change much. If anything, it suggests you're more concerned with my dog's welfare than you are with mine!'

'I'm here to do my job, not seek approval from someone like you.'

'Just as well,' said Flutter, 'because you totally failed on the approval front.'

'Are you going to behave or not?'

'I'm not going to give you an excuse to beat me up, if that's what you mean.'

Bright studied Flutter's face. He was a cocky sod right now, but Bright was confident he wouldn't be so sure of himself once he realised they had enough evidence to charge him. A knock on the door interrupted his thoughts.

'Stay here,' said Bright. 'I'll get it.'

He went to the front door and returned a moment later with Doris in tow. She looked wide-eyed as she came into the kitchen.

'What on earth has been going on?' she asked.

'You're here for the dog, aren't you?' said Bright. 'I'd appreciate it if you'd just take him and go. I need to get Mr Gamble to the police station.'

Doris stared open-mouthed at Flutter.

'I dunno what's going on, but I haven't done anything, Doris, honest,' he said.

CHAPTER 22

TWENTY MINUTES LATER, Flutter was sitting in an interview room trying to understand how his world had changed so abruptly and in such a short space of time. Across the table from him, Robbie Bright was feeling pretty smug as he flipped through his notes, and silently congratulated himself.

He felt things were going as well as he could have hoped. This was the first big case since he'd been at Waterbury, and he was keen to impress his new boss, DI Hammer. The fact that Flutter was their chief suspect was an unexpected bonus. Perhaps now he could convince Katie she was wrong about her new friend.

'If this is an interview, shouldn't I have a solicitor present?' asked Flutter.

'It's not an interview. You can see the recorder isn't switched on. This is an informal chat before my boss interviews you this afternoon.'

'Informal chat? What's that supposed to mean?'

'I'm just trying to make things easier for you.'

'Why? I keep telling you, I haven't done anything.'

Bright stared at Flutter, as if he could read his mind.

'You know, I knew you were going to be trouble the first time I set eyes on you,' he said.

'I thought, as a copper, you were supposed to look at facts, not prejudge people just because you don't like the look of them.'

'The thing is, there's a type,' said Bright. 'And you're it.'

'What you mean is, because you don't like me, I'm going to be prime suspect every time there's a crime.'

'What I'm saying is that there's a guy in hospital, and at the moment all the facts we have are leading us straight to you.'

'That's bullshit!'

'Is it? What can you tell me about a guy called Jed Rodgers?'

'Jed? He's the guy in a coma?'

'You know him, then?'

'Everyone who grew up in Waterbury back then knows Jed. When we were kids, he was the school bully.'

'You don't sound surprised he's in hospital.'

'From what I've heard, nothing's changed on the bullying front. Perhaps someone decided they'd had enough. It's not before time.'

'Does that mean you approve of what's happened to him?'

'I'm not saying that, but eventually, he was bound to pick on someone who wanted to get their own back.'

'Did you want to get your own back?'

'Who me? I was lucky enough to stay under his radar when we were at school.'

'What about since you came back to Waterbury?'

'I've not been back long enough to fall out with anyone,' said Flutter.

'Really? That's not what I've heard.'

'What have you heard?'

'We have a witness who says you had a fight with Jed in the car park behind the High Street.'

'It wasn't a fight,' said Flutter. 'He was treating his wife like a piece of shit, and I suggested someone should teach him how to treat her like a lady.'

'That someone being you, right?'

Flutter said nothing.

'You make a habit of interfering in domestic arguments, do you?' asked Bright.

'I do when I can see the woman is terrified and there's a thug who looks as though he's going to use his fists. What sort of bloke would I be if I let that happen in front of me and did nothing about it?'

'So, you told Jed Rodgers he should leave her alone?'

'Yeah, I did.'

'And that was all? Our witness claims something else happened.'

'You mean when Jed punched me in the face?'

'So, you admit you had a fight with him?'

'Don't I have to hit him back to make it a fight?'

'That depends. We heard you told Jed you were going to teach him a lesson. Only he was too quick for you, and he landed a punch while you were still thinking about it.'

'All right, so I'm not a fighter. He was much quicker than I expected, and I ended up on my arse. What about it?'

'You threatened to get even with him.'

'No, I didn't. It was the other way around. He told me he'd be coming after me to finish the job.'

'Tell me about his wife.'

'Tell you what about her?'

'Did you know her before this fight with Jed?'

'I didn't have a fight with Jed.'

'Whatever. Tell me about her.'

'I've known her since we were kids. She was my girlfriend when I was sixteen.'

'And I suppose you looked her up when you got back.'

'Why would I do that?'

'For old times' sake.'

'It was years ago. I didn't even know she still lived in the area, or what her number was, or anything about her.'

'But you got in touch with her?'

'Actually, no. She contacted me.'

'Why would she want to contact someone like you?'

'She's my probation supervisor.'

Bright raised his eyebrows.

'Your probation supervisor? Really? I didn't know you were on probation.'

'Nor did I until Jenny called me to tell me.'

'Isn't that sort of thing normally arranged before you leave prison?'

'I dunno. I've never been to prison before.'

'I think you'll find that's how it usually works.'

'That's why she had to call me. She said there had been some sort of admin cock-up but, as she knew me, they asked her to sort it out and smooth things over.'

'Smooth things over?'

'She said she would break me in gently. Make it easier for me to get started.'

'Break you in gently? How does that work?'

'We had our first meeting in Leslie's coffee shop.'

Bright guffawed.

'You're kidding me.'

'No, seriously.'

'You expect me to believe you had the first meeting with your probation supervisor in a coffee shop?'

'Yeah.'

'And what exactly happened at this meeting?'

'She went through all the rules and then I signed the paperwork.'

'What paperwork?'

'Whatever paperwork I have to sign. I dunno, I never read it.'

'But you've got a copy?'

'Now you come to mention it, no I haven't. She never gave me a copy.'

Bright sat back in his seat.

'Have you ever thought of writing fiction?'

'Fiction? What do you mean, fiction?'

'Well, come on. This whole probation thing is complete bollocks, isn't it?'

'What d'you mean, it's bollocks?'

'I have to admit you seem to have put some thought into your story, but you should have done a bit more research. I mean, there are so many holes it's laughable.'

'Why would I make it up?'

'Because you live in a sort of fantasy world. That's why you think you're a detective, isn't it? I think you got Jenny Rodgers to meet you in that coffee shop because you fancied trying it on with an old flame.'

Flutter couldn't understand what Bright was talking about.

'I told you, she contacted me. Ask her. She'll tell you it's all true.'

'I bet Jed found out and confronted you about it. That's the real reason he punched you in the face, isn't it?'

'When was he attacked?'

'Tuesday night, as if you didn't know.'

'Well, that proves you're the one making stuff up, mate,' said Flutter.

'I suppose now you're going to tell me you have an alibi?'

'As it happens, yes, I have. I was...'

Flutter suddenly remembered the promise he had made to Katie.

'Well, come on then, let's hear it,' said Bright.

'I'd rather not say.'

Bright laughed.

'You'd rather not say? Oh well, there we are, then. With a cast-iron alibi like that, a jury will be easily convinced of your innocence. You do realise "I'd rather not say" isn't recognised as an effective defence in court?'

'I don't need an alibi. I haven't done anything. You just have to ask Jenny Rodgers if what I've said is true. She'll tell you.'

Bright got up from his chair, walked to the door, opened it, and turned to face Flutter.

'I have asked her, you fool,' he said. 'That's how I know you're talking bollocks.'

He left the room, allowing a uniformed PC inside to watch Flutter, before closing the door firmly behind him.

Flutter was in a daze. He couldn't believe what he had just heard. Surely Bright must be bluffing. If he had spoken to Jenny, she would have confirmed his story, wouldn't she? And how could anyone think he would attack Jed?

CHAPTER 23

Robbie Bright was feeling good as he walked away from the interview room. He was certain they had the right man, and now he was going to leave him to sit in that interview room and let the reality of his situation sink in. Perhaps after an hour to reflect on the fact he was going back to prison, he might be a tad more co-operative for DI Hammer, who was surely going to be impressed with the efforts of his new DS.

In the meantime, Bright felt he had earned a cup of coffee, and half an hour with his feet up. As he made his way towards the canteen, his mobile phone rang. It was DC Brennan.

'Brennan? What have you found?'

He listened as Brennan explained.

'A baseball bat. In the garage? And there's blood on it? Fantastic! Well done, Brennan. I think you've hit the jackpot.'

Bright whistled happily as he slipped the phone back into his pocket and continued towards the canteen. He couldn't recall ever having experienced a more satisfying morning. The discovery of the baseball bat with blood on it would be perfect if the blood proved to be Jed's. If Gamble's fingerprints were on it too, that would truly be the icing on the cake!

A few minutes later, he collected a fresh cup of coffee from the canteen and carefully headed for his desk. He was just about to get settled in his chair when a voice called out.

'Detective Sergeant Bright. There's a woman down in reception says she needs to speak to you. She says it's urgent.'

'Tell her to come back later. I'm busy right now,' said Bright.

'I'm not your servant, Bright,' said the voice. 'You can come and tell her yourself, if you're brave enough.'

'I'm sorry?'

'Just so you understand, the woman in question is one very unhappy lady, and she's asked for you by name. Now, if you really want to piss her off even further, that's your choice, but you'll have to do it in person, because I'm not telling lies on your behalf.'

Muttering under his breath, Bright placed his coffee on the desk and made his way out to the reception area. Katie jumped to her feet as soon as his head appeared round the door.

'Why is Flutter here?' she demanded. 'What's going on?'

'I don't know what you're talking about.'

'Oh yes, you do. Doris, the dog sitter, told me.'

'I haven't got time for this now,' said Bright.

'Well, you'd better make some time,' said Katie. 'Because I'm not going away until I've got some answers.'

'You know I can't discuss an investigation with you. You're the press.'

'In this case, I think you'll find that's all the more reason to tell me what's going on. Unless, of course, you'd like me to jump to conclusions about the police victimising an innocent man just because he was recently released from prison. I can even think of one or two daily papers that would love to get their hands on a story like that.'

Katie's voice was growing louder and, to Bright's dismay, a small audience was surreptitiously gathering behind the reception desk. They hadn't made their minds up about the newest member of staff yet and were keen to see how he would cope with what appeared to be a potentially embarrassing situation.

'Keep your voice down,' he hissed.

'No, I will not keep my voice down,' she said. 'I've just been round to Flutter's house and seen the mess you've made. Was that really necessary?'

'Look, come on through and let's talk somewhere less public, can we?'

Without waiting for an answer, he led Katie through to an empty interview room and invited her to sit down.

'Right,' he said. 'I'll admit there was a bit of an accident in the kitchen, but these things happen sometimes.'

'I don't suppose PC Blackwell was involved with this "bit of an accident", was he?'

Bright hadn't expected her to know anything like that.

'Er, well, yes he was.'

'Of course he was,' said Katie. 'The man's a thug, and he hates Flutter. He would have been delighted with you giving him an excuse to smash the house up.'

'What d'you mean he hates Flutter?'

'They have history. Blackwell tried to arrest Flutter the day he came back to Waterbury.'

'Arrest him for what?'

'Basically, for inheriting a big house. Blackwell has a chip the size of a large boulder on his shoulder and a nasty attitude to match. You must have noticed by now.'

'I haven't had much to do with Blackwell, to be honest. Anyway, how come you know so much about him?'

'Much as I hate to admit it, he's my older brother.'

'Your brother? I've known you all this time and you've never mentioned you had a brother.'

'That's because he's not the sort of brother anyone would be proud of. Anyway, my family connections aren't important. What I want to know is, why is Flutter here?'

'I can't tell you that. As I said—'

'Yes, I know all the legal guff, but I'm not going to print the damned story, am I? Flutter works with me. I just want to know what's going on, and I want to stop you from making a complete fool of yourself.'

'Me? Make a fool of myself? There's a man in hospital, in a coma—'

'You mean Jed Rodgers?'

'You know about that?'

'Of course I know about that. It's a small town, and I'm the local press.'

'Yes, but—'

'You'd be surprised what I get to hear about.'

'So you know he was attacked and left for dead?'

'I heard he was attacked, but you can't think Flutter did that.'

'Why not?'

'He's not like that! He wouldn't hurt a fly.'

'Oh, really? I have a reliable witness who heard him say that, "Sooner or later, someone's going to give Jed a dose of his own medicine". How do you explain that?'

'Oh, come on, Robbie. That proves nothing. Jed Rodgers is a bully. Half the people in Waterbury would say the same thing if you asked them.'

'But he was almost beaten to death.'

'And why would Flutter do something like that?'

'He has a motive.'

'What motive?'

'He fancies Jed's wife, Jenny. She's an old flame and I think he was hoping he could rekindle the old romance. But she told Jed he was hassling her. That's why they had a fight.'

'When was this?'

'On Monday morning. Jed beat the crap out of him.'

'I saw Flutter on Monday morning. He had a bit of a bruise around his eye, but it was gone within a day or two. I'd hardly call that having the crap beaten out of him.'

'Jed made him look a fool.'

'And you think that would be enough for Flutter to bash his head in?'

'He didn't try, Katie, he succeeded.'

'And what does Flutter say about all this?'

'He says Jenny Rodgers is his probation supervisor, and that she contacted him out of the blue because the probation service had made a cock up. He says she arranged their first meeting in Leslie's coffee shop. I mean, have you ever heard such a load of rubbish?'

'I can vouch for that. I saw them together in Leslie's.'

'Ah, yes, but that was nothing to do with being on probation. He invited her for a coffee so he could test the water.'

'And you've spoken to Jenny Rodgers about this, have you?'

'As it happens, yes, I have. I hate to tell you this, Katie, but your jailbird friend is a pathological liar and a fantasist. I'm sorry, but I've told you all along that you shouldn't trust him.'

'And you've checked her out, have you?'

'I'm sorry? How do you mean, checked her out?'

'I'm assuming she's your witness.'

'Well, yeah. She was there when they had the fight.'

'But don't you think you should check her out before you take every word she says as gospel?'

'Well, of course we will, but—'

'So you haven't actually checked anything about her, or checked anything she's told you.'

'Well, no, not yet.'

'Oh, Robbie. You're going to look so stupid when Flutter's solicitor gets here.'

'What solicitor? He said he didn't want a solicitor.'

'Yes, I can imagine he did, but I can assure you there's a very good one on the way, and I intend to make sure Flutter gets to see him.'

This wasn't what Bright wanted to hear, and he knew DI Hammer wouldn't be impressed, either. There again, Flutter had a right to a solicitor, so he could do nothing to prevent it.

'What do you mean, I'm going to look stupid?'

'I'm not sure I know where to start,' said Katie. 'After all, I'm just an amateur playing at detectives. Isn't that what you said?'

'Get on with it, will you?' said Bright, irritably.

'Let's start with point one. Unlike you, the so-called professional detective, I did the amateur thing before I came here and made a quick search for Jed Rodgers' wife online. It turns out she isn't exactly as squeaky clean as you'd like her to be.'

'What's that supposed to mean?'

'She was working for the probation service until six months ago. They let her go because of who her husband is. They thought there was what you might call a conflict of interest.'

Bright beamed triumphantly.

'Ha! So there you are, then. She can't be his probation supervisor.'

'I agree. She can't be his "official" probation supervisor.'

Bright frowned.

'What do you mean, "official"?'

'You said yourself you thought the idea the probation service would work in such an ad hoc fashion was preposterous, right?'

'Of course it is.'

'You know that because you're an officer of the law, but what about Flutter? Would someone like him know how it all works? He's just come out of prison. He's trying hard to do everything right and terrified of putting a foot wrong. Would he ask questions if an old flame contacted him and said she was his probation officer?'

'Is there a point to all this?' asked Bright.

'I think you know what I'm suggesting, but as you've mentioned points, here's point two. If Jenny Rodgers isn't Flutter's probation supervisor, why did she call me and ask if I was employing him?'

'She what?'

'She called me, posing as his probation supervisor, on the pretext of checking his story about working for me.'

'You can't be serious.'

'I'm deadly serious.'

'When? When did she call you?'

'A week ago last Tuesday. First thing in the morning.'

'And you're sure about this?'

'Are you suggesting I'm lying? I think you know me better than that.'

Bright knew Katie wouldn't lie, but he couldn't believe Flutter's story was true. It made no sense, and of course, he still had his trump card.

'This is all very well, Katie, but how do you explain the fact we found a blood-soaked baseball bat in the garage at Willow Grove?'

'Has it got Flutter's fingerprints on it?'

'They're being tested as we speak.'

'I'll bet you anything you won't find his prints on the bat.'

'You're probably right. A guy like him would know to wipe it clean.'

'So you think he'd be clever enough to wipe his fingerprints off the bat but dim enough to leave it where you could find it, and with Jed's blood all over it? That sounds like a real master-criminal, doesn't it?'

'We all make mistakes,' said Bright.

'Yes, we do, and I'm trying to stop you from making a massive one right now. But I can't do that if you won't take those blinkers off and listen,' said Katie.

'But he's guilty!'

'No, he isn't, and you can't make him guilty just because you want him to be.'

'But he won't tell us where he was on Tuesday night. He's got no alibi.'

'Oh, but he has,' said Katie.

'So, why won't he tell me what it is?'

'The fact he won't tell you shows you the true measure of the man. He was with me on Tuesday night. The reason he won't tell you is that I made him promise he would never tell you.'

The colour slowly drained from Bright's face, and his mouth flapped wordlessly for a moment.

'With you? But, that's ridiculous.'

'Why is it ridiculous? What's wrong with me?'

'I don't mean it like that. He's not right for you. I told you that all along, and now you've—'

'Actually, no, we haven't. It's not what you think. We spent the night in a pub in a village called Felside in Cumbria, but I can assure you Flutter was the perfect gentleman.'

'Cumbria? What were you doing in Cumbria?'

'Playing at being Doctor Who.'

'What?'

'We went up there to interview someone. It was supposed to be a day-trip, but we got a puncture and couldn't get it fixed until the next morning, so we had to find somewhere to sleep for the night.'

A knock on the door ended the conversation.

'Yes,' shouted Bright.

The door opened enough for a constable to poke his head into the room.

'There's a solicitor in reception. He says his name's Harry Mackenzie, and he's here to represent your villain.'

'Tell him—' began Bright.

'No, you tell him,' said the Constable. 'He's raising merry hell out there demanding immediate access to his client, or else.'

'Or else, what?'

'I didn't ask him, but he doesn't look like the sort of bloke you want to keep waiting.'

Bright looked at Katie.

'He's right. It's probably not a good idea to keep him waiting,' she said, heading for the door. 'I'm sure the constable won't mind seeing me out.'

The constable's smile suggested he'd be thrilled to do so, and he held the door open for her. As she passed through the door, she paused and turned to Bright.

'That pub in Felside. It's called The Bull. You should call it. The landlord will confirm my story.'

As soon as she left the police station, Katie whipped out her mobile phone. She was sure Harry Mackenzie wasn't the name she had been told, but as she tapped in the number, she told herself that perhaps she had got it wrong.

'Bennet,' said a voice.

Flutter had only recently discovered Bennet was his uncle, and to his surprise his new found uncle had turned out to be one member of his family Flutter felt he could trust. Katie had her doubts about Bennet, but in the present crisis, she hadn't been able to think of anyone else she could turn to.

'It's Katie Donald.'

'Is Flutter all right?'

'I didn't get to see him, but I've put DS Bright straight on a few things. And that solicitor of yours, what's his name? Harry, is it? He's just turned up.'

'Who?'

'They said his name was Harry Mackenzie.'

'Harry Mackenzie? He's nothing to do with me. He's Jimmy Jewle's brief!'

'Oh, no, not him again,' said Katie. 'We thought we'd broken away from him. Can't you do something?'

'I can try, but I can't make any promises.'

There was a knock on the door of the interview room, and it swung open. A duty sergeant jerked his head at the PC, and he left the room as a slickly suited man entered carrying a briefcase.

'Who are you?' asked Flutter.

'Harry Mackenzie, at your service.'

'At my service?'

'I'm your brief.'

'I didn't ask for a brief.'

Mackenzie slipped into the chair opposite Flutter.

'No, they told me that outside. But you need one, you're entitled to one, and they don't come any better than me.'

'I can't afford a brief.'

'Don't you worry about that. It's all taken care of.'

'Taken care of?'

Alarm bells rang in the depths of Flutter's befuddled brain.

'Hang on a minute,' he said. 'If I didn't ask for you, that means someone sent you.'

Mackenzie beamed a smile at him.

'That's right. Jimmy sent me.'

'Jimmy sent you? Are we talking about Jimmy Jewle?'

'The one and only. You're lucky to have someone like that for a friend.'

'He's not my friend, and I don't want your help.'

'He won't be happy if he hears that.'

'I don't give a toss if he's happy or not. I don't want your help. You've had a wasted journey.'

'Are you mad? I've never met anyone stupid enough to say no to Jimmy Jewle!'

'Well, you have now,' said Flutter. 'I don't want you here, and I don't want your help, so you might as well clear off.'

'But what are you going to do?'

'I dunno, but I'd rather take my chances in a tank full of sharks than have Jimmy Jewle think I owe him a debt of gratitude. Now, are you going to leave, or do I have to get someone to throw you out?'

Mackenzie grabbed his briefcase and got to his feet.

'You'll regret this, you know.'

'I reckon I'll regret it more if I let you stay,' said Flutter.

'You could go down.'

'Like I said, I'll take my chances.'

Mackenzie stalked off, slamming the door closed behind him.

The PC returned to his station by the door.

'That was quick,' he said.

'Yeah, well, I'm not his man,' said Flutter. 'He was looking for someone to polish his boss's ego.'

CHAPTER 24

Robbie Bright kicked his wastepaper basket in frustration. It had taken a five-minute phone call to confirm what Katie had said about Jenny Rodgers and the probation service. Then another, even shorter call, to confirm that Mr & Mrs Gamble had stayed at The Bull, in Felside, on Tuesday night, and had two punctures repaired before they left, late on Wednesday morning.

In less than ten minutes, his entire case against Harvey Gamble had been reduced to tatters.

The phone on his desk was ringing, and he snatched it up.

'Yes!'

'It's Brennan. I'm at the lab.'

'Tell me you've got Gamble's fingerprints on that baseball bat.'

'I'm afraid not. It's definitely Jed Rodgers' blood, but there are no fingerprints.'

Bright swore colourfully.

'Crap! That's not conclusive evidence, is it?'

'But you said yourself Gamble knows what he's doing,' said Brennan. 'He would have known to wipe the prints off the bat.'

'Yes, but would he really be clever enough to do that and, be dim enough not to clean the blood off the bat, and leave it where we could find it?'

'I'm sorry, you've lost me,' said Brennan. 'I thought Gamble was our man.'

'I'm afraid we've got it wrong, Brennan. It's not Gamble, he's got a bloody cast-iron alibi.'

'Has he? Are you going to share?'

'He was in Cumbria on Tuesday night. He stayed the night in a pub so there's no way he could have got down here and attacked Rodgers.'

'Ah. That's not so good,' said Brennan.

'That's an understatement,' said Bright sarcastically. 'We're going to have to explain our mistake to DI Hammer.'

'We?' said Brennan. 'What do you mean "we" got it wrong, and "we" have to explain "our" mistake? I think it was you who insisted there was only one suspect.'

'But I was sure—'

'It was just after you spent an hour with that Rodgers woman, on your own.'

'It wasn't an hour.'

'It was fifty-six minutes if you want to be precise. I was sitting in the car, waiting. Remember?'

'What are you suggesting, Brennan?'

'I'm suggesting you were in charge, and I was just following orders. That means you're the one who needs to explain things to Hammer. You can leave me out of it.'

'What's Hammer like?' asked Bright. 'He's been on leave ever since I arrived. I spoke to him first thing this morning on the phone and I told him it was an open and shut case, and this afternoon's interview would just be a case of listening to the suspect's confession.'

'Well, if you don't mind me saying, overconfidence is never a good thing, and especially in front of someone like Hammer.'

'Why, what so special about Hammer?'

'You'll find out when you meet him. So, you'll have to let Gamble go, then.'

Bright sighed.

'Yes, I suppose so.'

'You can't keep him banged up if he's got an alibi.'

'Yes, yes. All right, Brennan. I know how the system works.'

'Actually, biting my head off won't make his alibi disappear.'

'I'm sorry. It's been a disappointing morning.'

'I suppose we'll have to start again,' said Brennan. 'Any ideas where?'

'Jenny Rodgers,' said Bright. 'She must have a reason for pulling my strings and leading me in the wrong direction.'

'D'you think a woman would be capable of that sort of violence?'

'I dunno. I suppose that would depend on her motivation. Whatever, I want you to pick her up and bring her here. Perhaps she can be the sacrifice to keep Hammer happy.'

'Right. I'll see what I can do,' said Brennan.

Bright put the phone back in its cradle, and quietly cursed his bad luck, but slowly, deep inside, he realised it wasn't bad luck that had created this mess. If he was being honest with himself, every decision he had made in this case had been driven by his almost pathological jealousy of Flutter and his relationship with Katie.

He had hoped his latest spat with Katie would end the way they always had before, but after his phone call with the landlord of The Bull, he knew it was going to be different this time. Hearing they had stayed the night in Cumbria as Mr & Mrs Gamble told him all his suspicions about Flutter and Katie had been correct.

He knew he should make sure Flutter was released, but a voice inside his head was telling him the prisoner could wait. He deserved to be punished for what he'd done with Katie.

The phone on his desk suddenly jangled into life, startling him from his moody thoughts.

'Bright.'

'That angry woman's down here again. She's asking for you.

Wants to know why you haven't released your suspect now you know he has an alibi.'

'Oh, does she now? Well, you can tell her—'

'You don't learn, do you? I told you last time. You can come down here and tell her yourself.'

There was a click as the line went dead. Bright looked accusingly at the handset, then put it down. Not for the first time that day, he wondered why on earth he'd moved to this stupid town. And why didn't anyone have any respect for him?

He sighed heavily and climbed to his feet. If Katie was making waves, he'd better go down and try to make the peace, and to do that, he guessed he'd have to release Flutter. This wasn't what he had planned, but perhaps if he swallowed his pride, he could at least salvage something that might improve his standing with DI Hammer.

'Why haven't you released him?' demanded Katie as soon as she set eyes on Bright.

'I was waiting to hear from forensics.'

'But why? Didn't I give him a good enough alibi? You checked it, didn't you?'

'I did. The landlord confirmed that Mr & Mrs Gamble shared a double room on Tuesday night.'

'It wasn't like that.'

'No. Of course it wasn't,' said Bright.

'Things aren't always what they appear to be.'

'Next you'll be telling me you didn't share a bed.'

'You wouldn't believe me, whatever I told you,' said Katie.

'I'd believe it if you told me you slept together.'

'You bloody hypocrite,' snapped Katie. 'What about you and Gloria Hadden?'

Bright's face turned a deep shade of red.

'What?'

'DC Gloria Hadden.'

'I don't know what you mea—'

'Don't play the innocent with me, Robbie Bright. You know exactly what I mean. You told me you were on a training course, but you forgot to tell me you were training her.'

'How did you f—'

'How did I find out? You made the mistake of humiliating my brother, so to get his own back, he called me to let me know what you'd been up to behind my back. It gave him the satisfaction of humiliating me as well as ratting on you, so thank you for that.'

'That bastard!'

'Well, I told you he was a shit. Now you know I meant it.'

'This doesn't make me any worse than you,' argued Bright.

'Of course it does. I didn't lie to you. Flutter and I went to Cumbria to do a job. We had a puncture and couldn't get back. If you had asked the landlord about the puncture, he would have confirmed it. Did you ask?'

'Er, yes, I did.'

'And what did he say?'

'He did mention something about two punctures.'

'Well, there you are, then. We didn't choose to stay the night, we had no choice. Anyway, I didn't come here to explain myself to you. What I do is none of your business. I'm here to give Flutter a lift home if you're ever going to let him go.'

'I am going to let him go, but before I do, I need your help,' said Bright.

'You want me to help you?'

'No, I want you both to help me.'

'You must be joking! I'm not sure I ever want to help you, and I doubt if Flutter will either, especially as you deliberately get his name wrong. Why do you do that? It's so petty!'

'All right, I admit I've messed everything up, and I shouldn't keep getting his name wrong, but if you help me, it will clear Flutter of all suspicion.'

'He shouldn't be under suspicion if you've confirmed his alibi.'

'But what about the baseball bat?'

'What about it?'

'It was in his garage, and it's got Jed Rodgers' blood on it.'

'But you know Flutter can't be responsible.'

'So, how did it get there?'

'We're just a couple of amateurs, playing at being detectives, remember? You're the professional. You work it out.'

'My boss is going to go spare,' said Bright.

'I don't think that's Flutter's fault, or mine.'

'Katie. Please!'

Katie studied Bright's face. She could see he was desperate, but even so...

'You don't need help, Robbie, you just need to take those blinkers off. What did you tell us about the old man in the cemetery?'

'The old man in the cemetery? What's that got to do with this?'

'When the old man collapsed, you said we were guilty of seeing what we wanted to see.'

'Yes, but—'

'Isn't that exactly what you've done here? You want Flutter to be guilty, so that's all you can see.'

'No, that's not true.'

'Yes, it is. You've wanted him to step out of line from the first moment you met him.'

'But the evidence—'

'I think you just need to ask yourself which battered wife pointed you in Flutter's direction.'

'Battered wife?'

'Oh, did she forget to mention that? Apparently, Jed knocks her around. Now, ask yourself, who has more motive for revenge than a battered wife?'

Bright looked suitably chastened. Katie was right. That sort of abuse could create a mighty powerful motive for revenge.

'Now, are you going to release Flutter?' she asked.

'Yes, of course. Come this way and I'll get it sorted.'

. . .

Twenty minutes later, Bright's phone rang.

'DS Bright.'

'It's Brennan. I'm at the Rodgers woman's house, but there's no sign of life. I'm wondering if she's done a runner.'

'Why would she run away if she thinks she's convinced us Gamble's guilty?' said Bright.

'Maybe she thought we might see through it and she planned on running anyway from the start,' said Brennan. 'Perhaps she set up Gamble so we'd waste a few days on him while she made a run for it.'

'Yes, that's a distinct possibility, but we've only just found out Gamble has an alibi, so there's no way she knows about it yet.'

'So?'

'So, my feeling is if she doesn't know Gamble has an alibi, she probably thinks she's got plenty of time, and she doesn't need to rush.'

'So she might still be in the area?'

'I reckon there's a chance, don't you?'

'What do you want me to do?' asked Brennan.

'Stay there for now in case she comes back. I'll get traffic monitoring the roads and I'll get onto the CCTV cameras in town. With any luck, she might not be too far away. I'll let you know if we locate her.'

CHAPTER 25

'I can't believe Jenny did that to me,' said Flutter, as Katie drove him away from the police station.

'You said you weren't the best judge of character,' said Katie.

'Not the best? I must be the worst in the world.'

'Look, don't beat yourself up about it. It's not your fault. She played you.'

'Yeah, she did. Rather too easily. I didn't realise I was so gullible.'

'Try not to think about it. You're free now. You have an alibi.'

'Yeah, about that. I'm sorry. I know you didn't want him to know.'

'Why are you apologising? I'm the one who told him. Why didn't you tell him from the start?'

'I promised you I wouldn't tell him.'

'But you had been arrested!'

'Yes, but I knew I hadn't done anything wrong.'

'Jenny had done a good job. She made sure there was a lot of evidence pointing at you.'

'But you did a better job. I can't thank you enough.'

'We've already been through that, and I told you, you don't have to keep on thanking me. I did what was right. You would have done the same.'

'No-one did that for me last time, you know. There were people I thought were friends who knew I was innocent, but not one of them came forward.'

'Yes, well, that was then. This is now. Maybe you were mixing with the wrong crowd. I look out for my friends.'

'And believe me, your friends truly appreciate it,' said Flutter.

'Well, now you're a free man. What do you want to do?'

'It's Friday, isn't it? I promised Doris I'd take her over to Willow Grove so she could collect the rest of her things.'

'Are you sure? After what you've just been through?'

'It'll give me something to do. Anyway, I like to keep my promises.'

Katie needed no more proof of that!

'Can I come?'

'It'll save me having to ask if I can borrow your car.'

'Does that mean I have to have your farty old dog in my car?'

'I'm afraid so, but he can sit in the back with Doris. She's used to the smell, and if you open the windows, you won't even know he's there.'

On the outskirts of Waterbury, Jenny Rodgers had stopped at the services to fill up her car with fuel and have a quick coffee break before she set off for the motorway. Jenny had promised herself she would join the motorway by 5pm so she had time to enjoy her coffee without rushing, confident that, so far, everything was going to plan.

It was strange to think it had all started, over a year ago, as a vague idea to get even with Jed. At first, she wasn't even sure she would ever have the courage to go through with it. But everyone has their breaking point, and Jenny reached hers six months ago when she was told she would have to leave her job because being married to Jed created a conflict of interest.

Her job made her life worthwhile and, after six months of brooding about losing it, Jenny decided it was time to get rid of Jed.

She had an idea how this might be achieved, but she first needed to find a fall guy.

When she saw Flutter in town one day, she felt fate was telling her he was the final piece of her jigsaw. Within minutes she had come up with an idea that would give her an excuse to contact him, and make use of the stationery she had kept back from her old job.

As luck would have it, Flutter was as uninformed as she had expected, and as soon as they met, it was obvious he was willing to rekindle their old romance. This was better than she had dared hope, but then she had always been able to twist him around her little finger.

She had expected it to take a few weeks or more to get everything in place, but after the visit to Flutter's house, she suddenly had almost everything she needed to set him up as her fall guy. She still couldn't quite believe he hadn't noticed her pocket his mobile phone, and he had actually handed her the access codes to the house in Willow Grove!

The missing piece of the jigsaw had been a believable motive, but Flutter had created that himself when he stood up to Jed in the car park. Jenny knew the police could be easily persuaded it was a sufficient motive for an attack.

Now everything was in place. All she needed to do was lure Jed into her trap. This was why she had stolen Flutter's mobile phone. She knew a message from that phone would be more than enough to goad Jed into a meeting, especially if he thought he it meant an opportunity to batter Flutter.

Of course, after the police informed her Jed had been found in a coma, she had first played the part of the distraught wife, and then been more than willing to help answer their questions so they might catch the culprit.

The gullible Detective Sergeant Bright seemed to have swallowed her story about Flutter, and he had already been arrested within two days of the crime being committed. She was confident that, once they searched the garage at Willow Grove and found the baseball bat soaked in Jed's blood, the police would believe they were onto a winner.

She knew from the fake probation terms she had induced Flutter to sign that he believed he was under a curfew so his only alibi would be that he was home alone the night Jed was attacked, and with no-one to verify it, he wouldn't have a leg to stand on. Of course, in his defence, Flutter would argue she had been lying, but by then there would be enough compelling evidence against him that it wouldn't matter what he said. And, even if they believed him, by then she would be far away.

As she took a sip of her coffee, Jenny looked at the clock on the car dashboard. She still had a couple of minutes before she needed to go, and there was something she needed to do before she left. She opened her bag and stared at the two mobile phones inside. One was Flutter's, which she had used to entice Jed to the meeting where she had attacked him. She intended to toss this phone from her car window when she drove across a bridge later that day.

It was the other phone that bothered her. She had always suspected Jed had a girlfriend, but had never proved it. However, this was a "pay as you go" phone she had found in his bedside cabinet. Although there was no name listed alongside the solitary number in the contact folder of the phone, Jenny was sure this had to be the phone he used to contact his girlfriend.

Of course, Jed wouldn't be cheating on her again, so the sensible thing to do would be to dump the phone in the nearest litter bin and forget about it. After all, knowing who the other woman was wouldn't change what had happened, would it?

A year ago Jenny probably would have done exactly that, but after all the months of brooding, she felt she needed to know she had been right about the existence of the girlfriend, and to know who she was.

She picked the phone from her bag and opened the contact list.

There it was, just the single telephone number. She stared at the number, wondering what she would say if the other woman answered. Then, after a few seconds of further hesitation, she pressed the call button but, before she could raise the phone to her ear, someone rapped their knuckles on the window alongside her. She turned to find a man's face staring at her and, startled, she dropped the phone.

At the same time, the passenger door opened, and another man climbed into the seat next to her. He was holding a warrant card out so she could read it, but she already knew this man's face.

'Detective Sergeant Bright,' she said. 'What are you doing here?'

'Hello, Jenny,' he said. 'Going somewhere?'

'I need to get away for a few days.'

'I'm sure you do,' he said. 'But I'm afraid it's not going to happen.'

He pointed to the officer on the driver's side, who was now opening her door.

'This is Detective Constable Brennan. We'd like you to come with us.'

'What for?'

'My boss, DI Hammer, has one or two questions he'd like to ask you.'

CHAPTER 26

At about the same time Jenny Rodgers was being arrested, Flutter and Katie were sipping tea in the kitchen of the house at Willow Grove. They had watched Winston having a wonderful time reacquainting himself with the garden, and now they could hear him snoring happily in his old bed. Doris was in the apartment above the garage fetching the rest of her belongings.

'Doris has been gone a long time,' said Katie.

'She's probably finding it difficult to say goodbye to the old place,' said Flutter. 'It was her home, don't forget.'

'But she's been up there for almost an hour now. How much stuff can she have in that flat?'

'I dunno,' said Flutter. 'I've never actually been up there. I don't like to rush her when she's upset about Alma being so ill. And she's been so helpful with Winston it would be ungrateful of me to have a go at her.'

'D'you think she's okay?'

Flutter looked at his watch.

'It's ten to five,' he said. 'If she hasn't appeared by five, I'll go and find her.'

There was a sudden noise; a dull, muffled, "whoomp."

'What was that?' cried Katie.

'It came from the basement,' said Flutter. 'The boiler's down there. Maybe it's just gone up the creek. I'll take a look.'

He made his way to a door under the stairs that led down to the basement. As soon as he opened the door, he instinctively slammed it closed again and ran towards Katie.

'The basement's on fire!' he shouted. 'We need to get outside!'

He rushed her out into the hall and out through the front door. They stopped on the forecourt to catch their breath.

'What on earth has happened?' gasped Katie.

Before Flutter could answer, another loud "whoomp" came from the garage. The metal door seemed to bulge momentarily, then crumpled and was left hanging uselessly. Flames could be seen from inside.

'Shit!' said Flutter, pointing to the windows in the flat above the garage. 'Doris is still up there.'

He raced to the garage where a fire escape staircase led up the side to the floor above, and round to a door at the rear, rushed up the stairs and hammered on the door.

'Doris! Doris! Come on, open the door.'

There was no answer from inside, so he ran back down the stairs and grabbed a brick from a small pile under the steps, then raced back up to the door. There was no time to mess around, so he smashed the glass in the upper part of the door, creating a hole big enough to get his hand through to open the door from the inside.

He found Doris in the bedroom, laying dazed, on top of the bed. In too much of a hurry to stand on ceremony, he scooped her up in his arms and dashed back to the door. Doris was wide awake now, as she was carried down the stairs, but she was bewildered.

Flutter wanted her as far from the house as possible, so took her down the drive to the gates. A shell-shocked Katie was waiting as he set Doris down. They could hear distant sirens.

'I've called the Fire Service,' she said. 'They're on their way.'

'I'll open the gates,' said Flutter.

'What just happened?' asked Doris.

'I think we've been fire-bombed, that's what happened,' said Katie.

'I think you mean Jimmy Jewle just happened,' said Doris.

'I don't understand,' said Katie. 'What makes you think Jewle had anything to do with this?'

'Before he left, he said he'd sent one of his men inside the house,' she said. 'He must have planted some sort of fire bomb.'

'But why would he do that?' asked Flutter. 'I told him I didn't want the house, and he was welcome to it!'

'I told you not to trust that man,' said Doris. 'He says one thing, then does the opposite. He's always been the same.'

'But the house won't be any good to anyone if it's a burnt-out wreck,' said Katie.

'You should have let me finish him while I had the chance,' said Doris. 'You'll have no peace now.'

'What d'you mean, we'll have no peace?' asked Flutter

'D'you really think a man like Jimmy Jewle is interested in this house, or money? He's got more than he could ever want. Why would he want more?'

'I'm not sure I follow.'

'All he really wanted was your father. He's been waiting over ten years to get his revenge, and a man can build a lot of resentment in that time.'

'What do you mean, revenge?'

'Your father humiliated him. No-one does that and gets away with it. He was probably planning on giving your dad a concrete overcoat. That's what he used to do.'

'Yes, but he's too late now. He can't get revenge on a dead man. No-one can.'

'You're right, he can't,' said Doris. 'But in Jimmy's head, the debt still has to be paid. Your father's not here, so he'll come after you instead.'

'No,' said Flutter. 'We parted on good terms. Burning this house down makes no sense.'

In the distance, sirens could be heard.

'This is Jimmy Jewle we're talking about,' said Doris. That means there is no way out. Trust me, he's not right in the head. He wants you dead!'

'So, if he wants me dead, why would he bomb this place? He knows I don't live here. And there's no way he could have known we'd be here this afternoon. We only decided to come a couple of hours ago.'

Doris narrowed her eyes and started looking all around as the siren sounds grew ever nearer.

'I don't know. Maybe he's watching the place,' she said.

'No, I'm sorry Doris, but I think you've got it wrong,' said Flutter. 'If Jewle had someone watching this place, he'd know I don't live here. And it would be a simple matter for him to find out where I do live. In fact, he probably knew that anyway, so why not set fire to that place?'

The sirens were almost deafening now, and they stood well back as the first fire engine turned in through the gates. A second followed close behind, but this one stopped outside. There was a brief period of what appeared to be total chaos as the fire engines disgorged firefighters in all directions. But, within a short time, hoses, ladders and assorted pieces of equipment were made ready, and the serious business of fighting the fire began.

One firefighter seemed to organise everyone else, and once he was happy, he came across to Flutter. He had to raise his voice above the noise and took his helmet off to hear better.

'Is there anyone inside?'

Flutter shook his head.

'No, there were only three of us in the house.'

'Well, that's a relief. My name's Phil Brown. I'll be coordinating the two teams. Is this your house?'

'Yes, it is.'

'Have you any idea what started the fire?'

'There was a sort of muffled explosion in the basement,' explained Flutter.

'Explosion? Is there anything inflammable down there?'

'Well, the gas boiler is down there, but nothing else that I can think of. As we ran out of the house, the same thing happened in the garage.'

Brown raised his eyebrows.

'Is there a boiler in there, too?'

Flutter shook his head.

'No. There is an apartment above the garage, but it's all electric. There's no gas over there.'

Now the firefighter scratched his head.

'And yet the same sort of explosion came from the garage? That's weird. You're sure there was nothing that might have started the fire?'

'This is going to sound crazy,' said Flutter, 'but I think someone might have planted some sort of device to start both fires.'

Brown took a step back.

'You think someone set your house on fire?'

'It's a long story, but yeah, I believe they may well have.'

'I can't let my lads go inside if there's a risk of further devices.'

Flutter's heart sank. He had already resigned himself to the fact the house would be severely damaged, but now it seemed it was going to be much worse.

'No, of course not,' he said resignedly. 'And, if I'm right, it's quite possible there could be more devices. I'd rather let the house burn to the ground than see anyone get hurt.'

'We'll control it as best we can from outside,' said Brown, ready to rejoin his team. 'I'd like you three to stay back here by the gates, well out of the way.'

Flutter watched as Brown slipped his helmet back on, then turned and ran back to his team. Katie stepped alongside Flutter and placed a hand on his shoulder.

'That's it, then,' he said, looking round at her. 'So much for my nice, big house. I knew, right from the start, that it was too good to be true.'

She patted his shoulder.

'But it could have been worse. At least no-one was hurt, and we're all still alive.'

'Yeah,' said Flutter. 'I need to speak to you about what Doris was saying.'

'I think you're right,' she said. 'Much as I dislike Jewle, he gains nothing by burning down the house. And if he really wanted you dead, there must be dozens of easier ways of doing it without killing all four of us at the same time.'

Alarm bells began clanging in Flutter's head.

'Four of us? Bloody hell. Winston! I'd forgotten about him. He was asleep in the kitchen.'

'You can't do anything for him now,' said Katie.

'I've got to try. I can't let the poor old thing die. None of this is his fault.'

She grabbed his arm.

'I can't let you do his, Flutter. Winston is almost certainly dead by now, and you will be too, if you go in there.'

'Trust me, Katie, if I don't do this, I won't have any peace for the rest of my life.'

'But this is crazy. You could die!'

He smiled and winked, then before she could stop him, he brushed off her hand and ran towards the house.

'Flutter, stop!' she screamed. 'Someone please stop him.'

She ran after him, then slowed down and breathed a sigh of relief as she realised one of the fire crew had seen him coming and was about to grab him. But then she let out a squeal of despair as Flutter easily side-stepped the man and ran off around the back of the house.

She tried to run even faster, but this time the firefighter was more alert. Although she tried to evade him, he caught her around the waist and easily lifted her off her feet, then carried her back towards the gates.

'You can't go round there, luv,' he shouted above the din. 'It's not safe.'

'But Flutter,' she said. 'You've got to go after him.'

Phil Brown had seen what happened and was rushing over.

'Where did he go?' he asked. 'I told him to stay well clear.'

'He just remembered his dog is in the kitchen,' explained Katie.

It was immediately apparent just how angry Brown was, and he swore expansively for several seconds before he spoke to her again.

'You mean to say he's risking his life for a bloody dog?'

'Please go after him,' said Katie.

'I'll send two lads around the back, but you need to understand we don't do suicide missions. The heat is intense, and the structure of the house has been compromised so much it might collapse. Your friend might have chosen to go inside, but I won't send my lads in there unless I can guarantee their safety.'

He indicated to two members of his team that he had a job for them. As they walked over, he turned to Katie.

'Now listen. This isn't a game we're playing here, so I need no more stupid behaviour, right?'

She nodded meekly.

'When Ray lets go of you, you're going to walk down to the gates and stay there. Got it?'

'Yes. Of course. I'm sorry.'

Phil nodded to Ray, who released Katie. She mouthed a thank you to him, then headed back to the gates, where another figure was now standing next to Doris. It was Robbie Bright. As Katie walked towards the gate, Bright rushed to meet her and swept her up in a bear hug.

'What on earth is going on?' he asked. 'Are you all right?'

'Take your hands off of me,' she yelled.

'But I was worried—'

'You might have been my boyfriend once, Robbie, but, in case you've forgotten, we're no longer an item. I'm not your girlfriend anymore.'

He set her down on the ground and released her.

'Okay, okay, I'm sorry.' He pointed to the blazing house. 'But look at this. Can you blame me for being worried? Where's Flipp — I mean, Flutter?'

She pointed at the house, every window now lit within by flames. Even the roof was now ablaze.

'If you must know, he's in there,' she said.

'Oh, my God. What happened? Did he get trapped?'

'His dog is in there. He's gone to see if he can rescue it.'

'Is he mad?'

'Yes, he probably is,' she said sadly. 'But I think what's happened to him over the last couple of days would have driven most people mad.'

'Look, we made a mistake, all right? I've said I'm sorry, but I'm not going to keep on apologising. Don't forget all the evidence pointed his way.'

Doris had been listening to the conversation, and now she was going to have her say.

'You're the one who arrested Flutter, aren't you? I thought I recognised you. You ought to be ashamed of yourself, thinking a nice boy like that would go around bashing heads in.'

'Do I know you?' asked Bright.

'You ought to,' said Doris. 'I'm the dog-sitter who came round to collect his dog.'

'Oh. So that was you, was it?'

'You're not very observant for a detective, are you?' said Doris. 'No wonder you arrested the wrong man. I bet you couldn't find your own arse with a map and both hands.'

Before Bright could think of a reply, there was a sudden shout from the direction of the house, and the three of them turned just in time to watch as, almost in slow motion, the roof of the house collapsed.

'Oh, my word,' said Doris, clutching hold of Katie. 'Where's Harvey? He's not still inside, is he?'

'I hope to God he's not,' said Katie fearfully.

Suddenly, there was a commotion from the side of the house and two fire officers appeared, supporting a man between them. The man appeared to be holding a dog in his arms, and as they watched, he bent down and released the dog, who waddled happily towards them, tail wagging defiantly, apparently unfazed by all the commotion.

'Oh my God,' said Doris, bursting into tears. 'He's alive. It's a miracle.'

Katie broke free from Doris' arms and ran across to Flutter, hugging him tight as the fire officers handed him over to her.

'Just make sure he pulls no more stupid stunts like that,' they said.

'Yes, of course,' she said, then turned her attention to Flutter.

'Are you okay?' she asked as she led him down to the gates.

'Yeah, I'm fine.'

'When the roof caved in, we thought you'd been trapped inside.'

'I didn't need to do the superman bit. Somehow, the back door had opened. I spotted Winston sniffing around in the garden as soon as I got round the back of the house. It's like a house fire is an everyday occurrence in his world.'

As they got to the gates, Flutter realised Bright was standing nearby, looking distinctly uncomfortable.

'What's he doing here?' he asked Katie. 'He looks like the proverbial spare whatsit at a wedding.'

'If you must know,' said Bright, who had caught Flutter's comment. 'I came here to let you know we've picked up Jenny Rodgers.'

'In that case, shouldn't you be back at the station questioning her?' asked Katie.

'Well, pardon me for showing some concern for your welfare,' said Bright.

'I don't need your concern,' said Katie. 'What I need is for you to find out what that woman has been up to, and why she tried to frame Flutter.'

'Don't you worry,' said Bright, angrily. 'That's what I'm going to do. I can see I'm not needed here.'

He turned on his heel and headed for his car.

'What was that all about?' asked Flutter.

'He's jealous,' she said. 'He thinks we're sleeping together.'

'I can understand why,' said Doris. 'I thought so, too.'

'What?' said Katie.

'Well, look at you,' said Doris. 'You're all over him.'

Katie let go of Flutter and stepped away, as if he were a hot coal.

'Nonsense,' she said.

'Is it?' asked Doris. 'Didn't you spend a night together in Cumbria?'

'Well, yes,' admitted Katie, 'but it wasn't like that. Flutter was the perfect gentleman.'

She turned to Flutter.

'Well, go on,' she urged him. 'Tell her there's nothing going on.'

Flutter shrugged and smiled, but said nothing. Embarrassed, he edged away and turned his attention to the house so he could admire the firefighters at work.

'Well, he's not going to say, is he?' said Doris.

'Why not?'

'Didn't you just say he was the perfect gentleman?'

'Well, yes, but why does that stop him from saying?'

'Because a perfect gentleman never tells,' said Doris.

'This is ridiculous,' began Katie.

'Why is it ridiculous?' asked Doris. 'He's a nice boy. You could do a lot worse, you know.'

Katie turned to Flutter for support, but Phil Brown had beckoned him over to explain something. When she turned back to Doris, she had settled on the low wall inside the gate and was making a big fuss of Winston, apparently satisfied she had won the argument.

Flutter had finished talking with Brown and made his way back to join them.

'He says there's not much we can do here,' he said. 'He's taken on board what we said about the fire being started by someone, and he's going to call in fire investigators.'

'So, what do we do now?' asked Katie.

'He suggested we might as well go home now and come back in the morning. They'll probably be here all night dealing with the fire.'

'I don't suppose there's any point in me coming back for the rest of my stuff,' said Doris sadly. 'It will all be charcoal by now.'

'Yeah. I'm sorry about that,' said Flutter.

'Don't be silly. It's not your fault.'

'That's not much help to you, though, is it?'

'You'll have enough to do sorting this lot out, without worrying about a few bits and pieces of mine,' said Doris.

'Yeah, that's a point,' said Flutter. 'I've never had to do anything like this before. I dunno where to start!'

'I can help you with that,' said Katie.

'Would it help if I took Winston home with me? I can keep him for a few days, if you like,' suggested Doris.

'That's a good idea,' said Flutter. 'Are you sure you don't mind?'

'I wouldn't have suggested it if I minded, now would I?'

'Thank goodness I didn't park too close to the house,' said Katie. 'Come on, I'll give you both a lift home.'

CHAPTER 27

SATURDAY

It was 07:30. It had taken most of the night to extinguish the fire and now, in the cold light of day, it was clear to see the top parts of the exterior walls had collapsed, leaving a sad, blackened shell surrounding the charred wreckage of the inside walls and floors. Thin tendrils of smoke wound lazily skywards as the weary firefighters gathered up their equipment ready to stow it back on the fire tenders.

Robbie Bright and Phil Brown surveyed the scene.

'Have you worked out what started the fire?' asked Bright.

'I can't say for sure until we've done a thorough investigation, and that won't happen until what's left of the building is made safe. But both fires seemed more intense than we would normally expect to see in a house fire. Add in the fact the owner said he thought some sort of fire bomb went off in the basement, and then something similar happened in the garage, and I can't see this being an accident.'

'So, if you can prove the fire was started deliberately, we could be looking at an attempt to murder the occupants?'

'We can only prove if the fire was started deliberately,' said Brown. 'The finer points around the intention behind it are down to you guys to prove.'

'When does the investigation start?'

'We must make sure the house is safe first. There will be a relief crew along to take over shortly. That will be their job. But if they give it the all clear, the investigation will start later today.'

He left Bright to his thoughts and headed off to help his crew finish clearing away their equipment.

Bright looked at what was left of the house.

'What a bloody mess,' he muttered.

'It's the story of my life,' said a voice.

Bright swung round to find Flutter walking up the drive to join him.

'You probably won't believe this, but I'm truly sorry about your house,' said Bright.

'Yeah, whatever. It is what it is,' said Flutter, gloomily. 'Anyway, what are you doing here?'

'I have a couple of questions I was hoping you might help me with.'

'You're kidding me, right?'

'Look, I know I made a mistake, and I understand how you feel about me right now. Honestly, I wouldn't ask if I didn't think it was important.'

'And you're not going to accuse me of something else?'

'Of course not. I just need you to look at something on my phone and tell me if you recognise it.'

Flutter sighed.

'All right, go on, then,' he said.

Bright found a photograph on his phone and showed it to Flutter.

'Does this belong to you?'

'Is that my mobile phone?' asked Flutter.

'I don't know,' said Bright, patiently. 'That's why I'm asking you.'

'Well, it certainly looks like mine. Is it?'

'Yes it is,' said Bright.

'Can I have it back?'

'Sorry, but no, not yet,' said Bright. 'I'm curious; most people have smart phones these days. How come you have this old thing?'

'You may find this hard to believe, but I get seriously pissed off with these people who can't live without being online 24/7. I prefer a phone to be a phone, rather than a permanent distraction. Anyway, where did you find it?'

'It was in Jenny Rodgers' handbag.'

'Really? What's she doing with it?'

'That's what we're trying to work out.'

'Did she use it to set Jed up?'

'Why d'you say that?'

'Because this is Jed Rodgers we're talking about. The man hates me. A text from my phone would be like a red rag to a bull.'

'Why did he hate you so much?'

'According to Jenny, he resented me because I was her first boyfriend.'

'That seems childish.'

At first, Flutter couldn't quite believe what Bright had said, but after what he'd been put through over the last few days, he'd just about had enough. He couldn't let this go without a response.

'That sounds rich, coming from you, Bright,' he said.

'What's that supposed to mean?'

'I suppose you think you've been a prefect example of the complete adult since I arrived on the scene, do you?'

'Well—'

'You're an idiot,' said Flutter. 'Katie's been great to me since I arrived in town, and I won't deny I do like her a lot, but there's no way I was going to muscle my way in between you two.'

'Yes, but—'

'You never gave me a chance, did you? You had it in for me from day one.'

'I wouldn't exactly say that—'

'That's why you were so keen to come and turn over my house, wasn't it? And that's why you brought Blackwell along. You knew he'd enjoy smashing my things.'

'That's not how it was.'

'That's exactly how it was, and you bloody know it. But, by not giving me a chance, all you did was show Katie how childish you were, and that pissed her off more than you'll ever know. And, as if that wasn't enough disappointment for her, you then went and cheated on her.'

'But she cheated on me.'

Bright was surprised at the desperation in his own voice.

'Only in your head, mate,' said Flutter.

'But she did. You know she did.'

'When? And who did she cheat with?' demanded Flutter.

'With you, of course. In Cumbria.'

'All that happened in Cumbria was we got a puncture, and when I tried to change the wheel, the spare was flat because Katie hadn't had her last puncture repaired.'

'That's what Katie said,' said Bright.

'Of course she did, because that's what happened.'

Bright said nothing for a few seconds as he struggled to regain his composure.

'This is irrelevant,' he said finally. 'And it's got nothing to do with my case. Where were we?'

'We were talking about Jed, and how people like him never really grow up,' said Flutter pointedly, happy to twist the knife a little more. 'And you didn't answer my question. Did Jenny use my phone to set Jed up?"

'We believe she used it to send him a text the night he was attacked,' said Bright.

'Which is what I said, right?'

'Yes, all right,' said Bright, unable to hide his irritation. 'But how would he have known it was from your phone? Did he know your number?'

'I dunno, but it wouldn't be hard to add my name to the end of a message, would it?'

'You told us you'd lost the phone. Do you remember when you lost it?'

'It's difficult to say. I don't exactly have a wide circle of friends so I don't use it much. Sometimes I go for days without using it at all.'

'Okay, let's try looking at it another way. Can you think how Jenny came to have it in her possession?'

Flutter thought for a moment.

'She could have picked it up when she was here last weekend.'

'You invited her here?'

'Not exactly. She invited herself. She said that, as my probation supervisor, it was part of her job to come and check out my house.'

'How did she get in? You said you don't live here, and there's a security system, isn't there?'

'Officially, I still own the place, so I still have access. I met her here and let her in. She told me we were going to have a meeting while she was here, and that it would kill two birds with one stone.'

Bright sneered.

'You really believed all that crap she gave you about being on probation, didn't you?'

'Why wouldn't I? I mean, I was only released a few weeks ago, and she seemed to know all about it, and she had all the proper paperwork. She even gave me a probation service business card with her name and number on it.'

'She really pulled the wool over your eyes, didn't she?' said Bright, keen to make sure Flutter feel as uncomfortable as he just had.

'Yeah, all right, so I was taken for a ride. But how was I supposed to know it was a con? I haven't seen her for years and I had no reason not to trust her.'

'And I suppose you still fancied her. For old times' sake.'

'I won't deny I did a bit, yeah. She's an attractive woman.'

'She says you made all the running.'

'I didn't make all the running,' said Flutter.

'Did she give you the come on?'

'I thought so.'

'I guess that makes sense,' said Bright. 'It would have made it easier for her to work her con if you believed there was a chance of having your way with her.'

'Did she plan all this while I was inside?'

'I can't say for sure. She claims she didn't even know you were back in Waterbury until she saw you walking your dog one morning.'

'Did she have an accomplice?'

'If she did, they must have communicated by smoke signals. They certainly didn't use any of the usual methods.'

'So, you think she was working on her own, and actually battered Jed herself?'

'We have to consider the possibility,' said Bright. 'You almost sound as if you hope she did.'

'Look, I have no time for people like Jed, but I wouldn't want to see him left in a coma. There again, he was a nasty piece of work, and I know he knocked Jenny about. It would be poetic justice if the battered wife turned out to be the one who stopped the career bully in his tracks, don't you think?'

Bright frowned.

'That's not how the system is supposed to work,' he said.

'I know that, but don't tell me you don't agree with me. You're just not allowed to admit it, right?'

Bright remained noncommittal.

'She had three phones in her bag,' he said. 'There was yours, her own, and an old-fashioned, unregistered one, like yours. You don't know anything about that, do you?'

'Are you trying to fit me up for conspiracy?'

Now it was Bright's turn to sigh.

'No, I'm not,' he said. 'I accept she was using you as the fall guy but, because of that, you're the only person who spent any time with her recently. I just wondered if you'd seen her with another phone.'

'I only ever saw her with her that fancy, all singing and dancing phone of hers, and there was only one number to call on the business card. I assumed it was the same phone.'

'Yes, it was,' said Bright. 'We've checked the number against your phone.'

'Well, there you go,' said Flutter. 'It looks as if I'm off the hook again.'

Bright refused to be drawn by Flutter's sarcasm.

'It's just that there was only one number in this unregistered phone's contacts, and she was making a call when we picked her up.'

'Well, if she thought I was still locked up, she was hardly likely to be calling me, was she?' said Flutter.

'I'm not suggesting she was trying to call you. I was just hoping you might have noticed something that would help me.'

'Well, I didn't, all right?'

Bright felt he had probably tried Flutter's patience sufficiently, and it was time to go.

'Right,' he said. 'Fair enough. Thanks for talking to me.'

Flutter sighed. He knew Bright was just doing his job, but didn't he have enough on his plate?

'Look, I'm sorry, but this just isn't a good time,' he said. 'Surely you can understand that?'

'I'm sorry,' said Bright. 'Of course I understand. I'll get off and leave you to it. You'll want to be kept up to date, though, right?'

'Sure, but give me a couple of days to get myself straight.'

'One more thing before I go,' said Bright. 'If this fire becomes a police matter, which it almost certainly will, I'll probably be part of the investigating team. So, you'll have to put up with me whether you like it or not.'

'Oh, terrific. I can't wait,' muttered Flutter, as Bright headed off down the drive.

Five minutes later, the relief crew arrived to relieve the firefighting team, closely followed by two fire investigators. They quickly took control of the site and began working to ensure the building was safe enough for them to start.

Flutter walked back down to the gates and sat on the low wall, gazing absently at the charred wreckage and wondering what he should do, and where to start. Then he was suddenly startled as someone slipped an arm around his waist and gave him a quick squeeze.

'How are you this morning?' said Katie, as she settled on the wall next to him.

'I feel better now you're here and your ex has gone.'

'Robbie? What was he doing here?'

'Now he knows he can't prove I tried to murder Jed, he wants me to help prove Jenny did it.'

'D'you think she did?'

'I wouldn't blame her.'

'Even though she tried to make it look as though you did it?'

'I admit I'm not too happy about that bit, but it didn't stick, did it?'

'Only because we were stranded up in Cumbria. If you'd stuck to Jenny's fake parole rules, you would have been home alone with no-one to confirm your alibi.'

'Yeah, that was a rare bit of good luck,' said Flutter. 'Perhaps I should share a bed with you more often.'

Katie looked sideways at him, but he stared resolutely at the house, giving nothing away.

'Don't start getting ideas,' she said.

'Who, me? I don't know what you mean.'

'You know perfectly well what I mean. Anyway, what about the house? Do they know what started the fire?'

Flutter nodded towards the house.

'Those guys haven't finished making it safe yet, so they haven't started investigating.'

'I had a call from Bennet this morning.'

'Bennet? He called you?'

'He said he didn't call you because he thought the police might still have your phone, and it might take some explaining.'

'He's my uncle, and my house has just burnt down. Why shouldn't he be calling me?'

'No reason at all. He just doesn't think the police would see it that way.'

'If they look hard enough, I'm sure they'll find his number in my call history,' said Flutter.

'They've got no reason to be looking through your call history.'

'Yeah, right. That doesn't mean they won't though, especially if Robbie Bright has anything to do with it. Anyway, you were saying Bennet called.'

'Apparently, he has his sources.'

'Bloke's like Bennet find it pays to keep their finger on the pulse. That way, they know if there's a problem heading their way.'

'Well, it turns out one of his sources told him someone had been looking to buy materials to make a fire bomb.'

'Now there's a coincidence,' said Flutter.

'That's what Bennet thought when he heard about the fire.'

'So, come on, whose the phantom arsonist?'

'The word is it was your friend Jed Rodgers.'

'Jed? That's a bit sophisticated for a moron like him.'

'There are plenty of videos online that show you how to make these things,' said Katie.

'Yeah, I suppose there are. But how did he detonate them if he was in hospital?'

'A timer?' suggested Katie.

'Set days in advance? How could he have known we were going to be in the house?'

'Perhaps he just wanted to destroy the house, and we weren't supposed to be there.'

'Hmm, maybe, but I dunno. Forward planning has never been Jed's thing. He's more of a plant the bomb, light the fuse, and run, sort of bloke.'

'What about a remote detonator?'

'Sorry?'

'I don't know how you make them, but you can create a detonator circuit from a mobile phone that's triggered by a call from another mobile phone. You can be miles away, and as soon as it rings, the circuit completes, and boom!'

'And how does Jed make the call when he's in a coma?'

'What if he had an accomplice? And what if it was Jenny? Maybe she planted the bombs when she was here last Saturday.'

'Katie, she brought nothing into the house with her, and she never left my sight. And why would she want to burn the garage down? That's where she planted the baseball bat.'

'Oh, yes. I hadn't thought of that. But what if the plan was to start the fire once she knew they'd found the bat?'

'How would she know? And anyway, even if she knew, what would she gain by burning the place down? And why would she help Jed do anything? Remember, she hated him enough to try murdering him.'

'Perhaps she felt she had no choice.'

'But he can't make her do anything now, can he?'

'Why are you defending her?'

'Because, if you ask me, her starting the fire makes no sense.'

They sat in silence for a minute or two until Flutter spoke again.

'Look, I don't know about you, but I find sitting here staring at this mess seriously depressing. There are things I need to sort out, and I don't have a clue where to start. Will you help me?'

'Of course I will,' said Katie, with a sad little smile. 'We should probably contact your insurance company first.'

'Insurance company?'

'To report the fire. The house is insured?'

Flutter looked horrified.

'Oh, Flutter,' said Katie. 'Don't tell me the house isn't insured.'

'The thing is, I know nothing about insurance and stuff. I've never had a house before so I've never needed to... I just assumed...'

Katie slipped her arm around his waist and gave him a consoling squeeze.

'Have you kept all the documents that came with the house?'

'Documents? Well, there's the letter I was sent.'

'I suppose that will have to do for a start,' said Katie. 'Come on, let's see what you have, and what we can find out. There's nothing we can do here, anyway.'

CHAPTER 28

WEDNESDAY

It was Wednesday morning. Katie and Flutter were drinking coffee in his kitchen. It had been four days since Katie had started trying to discover the insurance status of the house in Willow Grove.

'I think we're going to have to accept the fact the Willow Grove house wasn't insured,' said Katie.

'I'm sorry,' said Flutter. 'It just didn't occur to me...'

'You have insured this house now, haven't you?'

'Yeah. I did it Monday when you told me to.'

'Well, I suppose that's something,' she said.

'Don't be like that, Katie. I didn't do it on purpose. I just didn't know.'

'I know you didn't do it on purpose. But you know this means you won't be able to rebuild the house, don't you?'

'That doesn't worry me so much,' said Flutter. 'I didn't want the house anyway. What concerns me is what Jimmy Jewle is going to say. I did tell him he could keep the house, remember?'

'But I thought he told you he didn't want it and you could keep it.'

'Yeah, but it was all bit up in the air. I'm not exactly sure what we agreed in the end. And who knows if he'll keep to any agreement anyway.'

The sound of knocking on the front door echoed through the house.

'I'll get it,' said Katie.

'Tell whoever it is we don't want any today,' said Flutter, gloomily.

Katie opened the front door.

'Katie?' said Robbie Bright. 'I didn't expect you to be here.'

'I'm here supporting my friend,' she said. 'He's had a bad few days.'

'Right. Yes, of course.'

'What do you want, Robbie?'

He produced a folder from under his arm and held it up for her to see.

'I've come to see Flutter. It's about the fire investigation.'

'Have they reached a conclusion?'

'More or less. It'll take a while to finalise it, but they're confident they know what happened. I promised Flutter I'd keep him in the loop.'

'You'd better come in, then,' said Katie.

Bright stepped carefully into the house and waited while she closed the front door.

'Flutter's through here,' she said, leading Bright to the kitchen.

'Morning, Flutter,' said Bright. 'How are you?'

'I've been better,' said Flutter. 'Have you come to give me my mobile phone back?'

'I'm afraid we're going to have to hang on to that for now. It's evidence, you see. I can try to—'

'Don't worry,' said Flutter. 'I thought you might need it so I bought a new one.'

Bright waved his folder in the air.

'I'm here to let you know the outcome of the fire investigation.'

'My house burnt down,' said Flutter. 'That was the outcome.'

'Well, yes, there's no denying that,' said Bright. ' But I'm here to tell you what caused the fire, and who caused it.'

'Go on then. Let's hear it,' said Flutter.

'Can we sit down?' asked Bright.

Flutter pointed through to the lounge.

'In there,' he said.

Once they were settled Bright began.

'Right, well, when we checked to see if the house was insu—'

'It wasn't insured,' said Katie. 'So that rules out Flutter as a suspect, right?'

'Me?' said Flutter.

'Their first thought would have been an insurance fraud,' Katie explained. 'You burn the house down and collect the money. Except the house wasn't insured so you'd gain nothing.'

Flutter looked at Bright who shifted uncomfortably in his chair.

'Is that right?'

'It's something we always have to consider,' admitted Bright.

'And, I suppose, as it was me, you gave it extra consideration,' said Flutter.

'Look, it's routine,' said Bright. 'People normally insure their houses.'

'Well, I didn't,' said Flutter. 'And don't ask me why. I've been asking myself the same question for the last three days, and the only conclusion I can draw is that it's because I'm stupid. I don't need you telling me you agree. Let's just forget that bit, and move on.'

'Okay. Whatever you say,' said Bright.

He opened the folder and stared down at its contents for a moment to hide the smile that was threatening to break out across his face.

'Right,' he said. 'The investigators found traces of accelerant at the source of the fires in the basement and in the garage. They also found pieces of what they believe are mobile phones. Their belief is—'

'—that the fire bombs were triggered remotely,' finished Flutter.

Bright was visibly taken aback.

'You know this?' he asked.

'We thought as much,' said Flutter. 'It was either that or some sort of timing device, but that seemed more unlikely.'

Bright looked quizzically at Katie.

'"We" thought as much?'

'Not too shabby for a couple of amateurs, eh?' said Katie.

Bright sniffed

'Humph. Anyone could have guessed as much,' he said, grudgingly. 'The bigger question is, who made the bombs, and who planted them?'

'Jed made them,' said Flutter.

'How d'you know that?' asked Bright.

'Rumours,' said Katie.

'Rumours?'

'You can hear all sorts of things if you know who to ask, and where to listen.'

'Are you two sure you know what you're getting into?'

'Don't you worry, Robbie. We're just fine, thank you.'

Bright shot her a dirty look, then continued speaking.

'We've had a tip off that Jed Rodgers was looking to buy the materials to make fire bombs. We know he also bought three cheap mobile phones. And we know he's been online watching videos about bomb making.'

'There you go then,' said Flutter. 'All the necessaries to make, and remotely detonate, two fire bombs. The only thing I don't get is how he managed to get in and plant them.'

'Ah! I might be able to help you there,' said Bright.

He produced a clear evidence pouch from his folder.

'I can't let you touch this,' he said, 'but you can see it well enough.'

'What is it?' asked Katie.

'It's a piece of paper we found in one of Jed's pockets. It's got some numbers written on it.'

He handed it to Flutter.

'Do those numbers mean anything to you?'

Flutter recognised the numbers straight away.

'These are the security codes to the house,' he said.

'We thought they might be,' said Bright. 'We don't recognise the handwriting though.'

'It's mine,' said Flutter, guiltily. 'I wrote the numbers down because I can't always remember them. I gave the paper to Jenny in case she needed somewhere to hide from Jed.'

'And you're quite sure that's your writing?'

'Yeah, definitely,' said Flutter.

'Then I'm afraid it looks like she passed it straight on to Jed,' said Bright.

'I can't believe she did that,' said Flutter.

'She denies it, of course,' said Bright. 'She claims Jed often went through her bag and he must have found the piece of paper. But how would he have known what the numbers were if she didn't tell him?'

'He knew she'd been to the house,' said Flutter.

Bright looked sceptical.

'Perhaps he did, but that doesn't explain how he knew these numbers were the security codes unless Jenny told him. Either way, it explains how Jed gained access to the house so he could plant the bombs.'

Flutter remained unconvinced.

'I still don't see how he could have made the call to trigger the detonators when he's in a coma.'

'That's why we're convinced Jenny was his accomplice.'

'How does that make any sense?' asked Flutter.

'Why not?'

'Are you suggesting she had nothing to do with the assault on him?'

'Oh, no. We're quite confident she lured him into a trap and then battered the crap out of him with a baseball bat.'

'So, why would she help him, after that?'

'You said yourself he used to beat her up, and she was terrified of him.'

'So you think she hated him enough to try and murder him, but at the same time felt she had to set off his bombs?'

'Well, yes, I suppose I am.'

'That's a bit of a shit argument, isn't it? I mean, he was in a coma! What's he going to do to her if she doesn't make the call? What's her motive, if there's no fear of Jed coming after her?'

'To get at you, of course.'

'But as far as she knew, I was sitting in a cell waiting to be charged with attempted murder. What would she gain by burning down my house?'

'Rubbing salt in the wound.'

'She's admitted all this, has she?'

'She's not going to admit it, is she?' said Bright. 'She's in enough trouble already.'

Flutter shook his head.

'No, I don't believe it,' he said.

'All right, what time did the fire start?' asked Bright, turning to Katie.

'Just before 5 pm,' she said. 'I remember Doris had been gone a long time and I was wondering where she'd got to. Flutter looked at his watch and said he'd give her ten more minutes, and then it would be 5 o'clock. If she didn't appear by then he said he'd go and find her.'

'Then what happened?'

'There was a loud noise from down in the basement.'

'Right,' said Bright. 'When we found Jenny Rodgers in her car, she was making a phone call. According to the phone, the call was made at 4:55 pm. There was only one number in the contact list, and we believe it was the number that triggered the first bomb. It also triggered the second one which had a timed delay built into the detonator so it went off a few seconds later, in the garage.'

'I still don't believe it,' said Flutter.

'I get it that you don't want to believe it of your old girlfriend,' said Bright. 'But I'm afraid those are the facts, and it's all backed up by forensic evidence.'

'Did you ask her about it?'

'Of course we did. She maintains she found the mobile phone in a drawer at home. She thought Jed had a girlfriend and assumed this was the phone he used to contact her. She claims she was calling the girlfriend to find out who she was.'

'Well, there you are, then,' said Flutter. 'It was an accident.'

'Except the number she called is that of one of the three mobile phones Jed bought just last week.'

'So it was the trigger,' said Katie.

'Exactly,' said Bright. 'On top of that, we've found no evidence to suggest Jed had a girlfriend, so her story sounds like the lame excuse I believe it is. I hate to say it, but I'm afraid Jenny Rodgers is a devious, mean-minded woman who attempted to murder her husband, and came close to killing three people at 54 Willow Grove.'

'What's going to happen to her?' asked Katie.

'It's not up to me, but I would imagine she'll be charged with four counts of attempted murder, at the very least,' said Bright.

There was little more to be said, so Bright made his excuses and left them to their thoughts.

'Well, I got her all wrong, didn't I?' said Flutter. 'I told you I was a hopeless judge of character. I mean, there were moments, when I was alone with her, that I thought I might even have a chance of turning the clock back.'

'You mean to rekindle your old romance?' suggested Katie.

'Yeah.'

'I think it's fair to say you and Jenny were at cross purposes there, don't you?'

EPILOGUE

Two Weeks Later

It was almost as if learning the truth about Reggie was all Alma had been waiting for, and within days of Flutter and Katie explaining everything to her, she had passed away.

Now Katie, Doris and Flutter were standing outside the crematorium, watching as Alma's coffin was carried inside from the hearse. Flutter hadn't attended many funerals but he hated everything about them.

They made him so sad he always shed a few tears, and watching Doris and Katie putting on brave faces only made him feel even worse.

As he turned away to brush a tear from his cheek, he thought he must be seeing things, or perhaps the tears were distorting his vision. But when he wiped his eyes, the vision was still there.

He reached out and gently touched Katie's hand. She turned a quizzical face up at him.

'Look,' he whispered, gazing to his side. 'They must have come to see her off.'

Katie followed his gaze, then raised a hand to her mouth and let out a tiny gasp of surprise, as she saw about twenty ducks filing silently past behind them.

'That's spooky,' she said. 'Where did they come from?'

'I dunno,' he said. 'It's the perfect send off, though, don't you think?'

Katie gently nudged Doris.

'Look behind you,' she said. 'Flutter says they must have come to say goodbye to Alma.'

Doris turned to watch as the ducks continued silently on their way, finally turning a corner and disappearing, one by one, behind a small building opposite. When they had all gone, Doris turned back to face the front.

'Alma would have enjoyed that,' she said. 'She always had a soft spot for ducks.'

DID YOU ENJOY THIS BOOK?

You can make a big difference

I hope you have enjoyed reading this book. Reviews are one of the most powerful tools in any authors arsenal when it comes to getting attention for books, and I'm no different. A full page ad in a daily newspaper would be great, but that's just a tad beyond my budget!

But I do have something equally powerful (probably more so), and that's a growing bunch of loyal readers.

Honest reviews of my books help to bring them to the attention of new readers who will, hopefully, go on to join this growing band.

If you've enjoyed this book and you can spare a few minutes, why not leave a review? It doesn't have to be War and Peace, just a few words will do!

Click here if you'd like to help

ALSO BY P.F. FORD

Slater & Norman Mystery Novels

Death by Carpet

Death by Plane

Death by Night

Death by Kitchen Sink

Death by Telephone Box

Death in Wild Boar Woods

West Wales Murder Mysteries

A Body On The Beach

A Body Out At Sea

A Body Down The Lane

A Body At The Farmhouse

A Body In The Cottage

A West Wales Sequel

A Date With Death

Donald & Gamble Mysteries

In Need of Closure

At Cross Purposes

Dave Slater Novellas

An Innocent Victim

ABOUT THE AUTHOR

Having spent most of his life trying to be the person everyone else wanted him to be, P.F. (Peter) Ford was a late starter when it came to writing. Having tried many years ago (before the advent of self-published ebooks) and been turned down by every publisher he approached, it was a case of being told 'now will you accept you can't write and get back to work'.

But then a few years ago, having been unhappy for over 50 years of his life, Peter decided he had no intention of carrying on that way. Fast forward a few years and you find a man transformed. Having found a partner (now wife) who believes dreamers should be encouraged and not denied, he first wrote (under the name Peter Ford) and published some short reports and a couple of books about the life changing benefits of positive thinking.

Now, happily settled in Wales, and no longer constrained by the idea of having to keep everyone else happy, Peter is blissfully happy being himself, sharing his life with wife Mary and their three dogs, and living his dream writing fiction.

You can follow P.F. Ford here:
https://www.pfford.com

Printed in Dunstable, United Kingdom